HARD LUVIN' STRAIGHT THUGGIN' 3

A SOUTHSIDE LOVE

S. YVONNE

SHAN PRESENTS, LLC

Hard Lovin' Straight Thuggin' 3
Published by Shan Presents
www.shanpresents.com

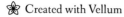 Created with Vellum

SUBSCRIBE

**Text Shan to 22828 to stay up to date with new releases,
sneak peeks, contest, and more....**

WANT TO BE A PART OF SHAN PRESENTS?

To submit your manuscript to Shan Presents, please send the first three chapters and synopsis to submissions@shanpresents.com

PREVIOUSLY

I gave Messiah another weak smile and then wrapped my arms around him although I knew he didn't want me to. I felt his body tense up. "Hug me Messiah." He refused.

"Give him some time." Qui said again. I let him go... that was one of the most fucked up feelings ever cause I knew at one point he loved the shit out of me. I knew he still did no matter how he tried to hide it cause if he didn't... then why didn't he tell my family my secret. Who was he tryna protect, them or me?

I walked away and allowed them all to follow me to the lobby where Bambi and Pete were still waiting. I glanced over to Messiah and Qui wondering what kind of conversation they were wrapped up in before deciding to go and use the restroom to take some pressure off of my bladder. By the time I walked out, the staff was ready for me. "You all can wait right here while we take her back first, and then once she settles in we'll allow you back to see where she'll be staying." The beautiful woman told them. I assume she'd be my nurse or something of that nature although she didn't wear scrubs, or maybe she would be my counselor. I thought to myself. Yeah, that's it... a counselor.

She led me to an plain white door and opened it. Behind the door was a simple twin bed that was made up perfectly with a rocking chair in the corner next to two windows. There was a fluffy rug on the floor and a few other things but nothing major. One thing I did notice was there was absolutely nothing in the room that I could use to harm myself with... not that I wanted to harm myself anyway, but I guess that was just proper protocol and I understood. The lady who wore a simple royal blue collared shirt, with a pen skirt and the matching heels smiled at me. Her smile was so welcoming. Her jet-black hair was short and curly and her pale white skin didn't even have one blemish on it. A pretty soft colored pink lipstick covered her lips and her teeth wore a set of braces when she smiled. "This is where you'll be staying okay sweetheart?"

I nod my head and gave her a weak smile.

"Now before we go over everything I'm gonna allow you to speak with your family before they leave and you can let them see exactly where you'll be staying so they can have some kind of comfort in knowing you're comfortable. After that, we discuss everything pertaining to you so that you can have an better understanding of this program; your family knows, but you need to know as well."

"Thank you very much."

"By the way." She extended her hand. "I'm your counselor Ms. Reynolds but you can call me Pam if you like. What should I call you? I saw in the chart that you have two names you go by."

"Well yes, my real name is Belcalis, but I prefer to be called Bari."

She smiled again. "Okay... Bari will do. Where did you get the nickname? If you don't mind me asking?"

With sadness overwhelming me, I told her the truth. "I got it from my cousin Ronnie because he hated calling me Belcalis... but he's deceased now."

"Oh I see... well I'm very sorry to hear that Bari. I'm sure he'd be proud of you if he was still here."

I cleared my throat. "Can you have Pete to come back first and then the rest of my family?"

"Sure... no problem."

I took a seat on the edge of the twin bed that would be mine until whenever I decided to leave this place. Technically I was here on my own free will so they couldn't hold me against my will. "Hey..." Pete got my attention causing me to jump since I was so wrapped up in deep thought. He sat next to me with an disturbance on his face.

"Hey... " I mumbled. "So this is it huh? Ya'll throwing me to the wolves."

He lightly chuckled, "Yo ain't nobody throwing you to no wolves shorty. You here cause we care about you... you know that."

"Yeah, I know."

He didn't say anything else so I continued on. "You gonna get another girlfriend while I'm gone?"

"Come on Bari, that's the last thing that should be on yo mind."

Something was off with Pete and I felt it. "Pete what's wrong?"

"I'm not even sure if I should address it to be honest with you. Like, honestly, I don't know what the fuck to think cause by default I kinda heard some shit just now that I really didn't wanna hear."

I swallowed hard wondering what he was even talking about but right now wasn't the time for him to bail out on me... I really needed him at this point. "Let's talk about it."

He stood up and walked to the window, putting his hands in his pocket. Wiping his hand across his waves, he took a long deep sigh. "Yo, just give me a minute aiight?"

I walked closer to him and stood directly next to him staring out at nothing particular. I really hoped that he wasn't about to break up with me cause I couldn't do this without him, on God I couldn't. it was crazy how me starting off by using him turned into me feeling like now a day couldn't go by without him. While Tuff would probably always be somewhere in my heart, the feelings that I was developing for Pete was something that I couldn't explain. I just knew he showed me a love I never felt before. "Pete please." I whispered. "I cant take the agony."

"Mayne, I over heard a conversation with Gu and his girl not too long ago and I swear I wasn't eaves dropping but it's like, it was meant for me to hear the shit Bari."

I furrowed my brows as sweat trickled down the sides of my face. "What conversation?" I questioned noticing how shallow my breathing became and his too.

"Yo... you got a lot of secrets ma."

"Pete!" I cried. "Please just say it, I can't take it... please." I knew what he wanted to know and I was ready for him to ask so I can get it out of the way. I had to free myself... I just had to.

He turned and looked directly at me giving me a side-eyed look. "Yo be honest with me Bari... is that my baby you carrying?"

My eyes dropped along with my heart, just when I thought I could answer him, I couldn't.

"Guess that answers my question...." He dropped his head. "Damn!"

"Pete..." I grabbed his arm. He snatched back, "yo don't fuckin' touch me right now Bari, on the real don't fuckin' touch me!" the tears fell down his eyes, and that hurt me more than anything.

"I'm sorry Pete... but please don't do this right now, I need you."

"Fuck that Bari, you got a lot of shit goin' on and you need to be honest with everybody including yo mama first!"

"I can't hurt my mama like that right now! I'm not tryna hurt my mama like that Pete! You don't understand!" I cried.

"Tell her Bari!"

"Pete I can't!

"I'm telling you! If you don't tell her... I'mma tell her. You gone tell Sue today... right now! Or I promise you it's on!"

"Pete... pleaseeee!" I begged.

"Tell me what?" Sue asked from the door looking at both of us suspect. "What's going on Bari?"

I was stuck.... just when I thought I was ready to move on and face these challenges, I was fucking stuck. Now I was about to lose Pete too. How fucking stupid can I be? As if I needed anything else...

my whole family was now standing behind Sue waiting for me to release my demons. May the Lord be with me.

To be continued......

ONE

Belcalis (Bari) Carter

My heart raced at a pace I didn't even know existed. "Pete pleaseeee!" I focused on him instead because I couldn't look at Sue. I couldn't stomach the displeased look on Messiah's face either as he stood with Qui to his side. Becka... the look from Becka scared me. What would my favorite and only aunt do if she knew the truth? My granna... how could I hurt her in this way? She didn't raise us up like this. I was her first and only granddaughter and in her eyes, I was a saint. I felt Bambi rush to my side for support as she gently squeezed my hand. Looking up in Pete's eyes with regretful tears of my own... I just wished there was something in him that would forgive me and make him understand. I dropped my eyes. "Please." I said in a whisper.

"Pete! What the fuck happened?" Sue eased away from the door inching her body closer to ours while shooting daggers. "What is Bari hiding?"

I gripped Pete's hand a little harder, my way of silently begging. He didn't remove his hand this time, he simply addressed Sue.

I saw the long deep sigh that he tried to disguise before saying anything to her. "Um Sue, I know I haven't had that many interactions with you... but I was damn sho looking forward to it thinkin' that Bari was gone be my girl fo' life and all, but I'ma let her explain why she just missed out on a good nigga." This time he removed his hand from mine and adjusted his fitted cap. "I've got my own problems to deal with aiight? Ya'll take care." He stepped around the three of us without even looking back.

My knees involuntarily hit the floor, throwing both my hands to my face, I sobbed in misery. Bambi stood there looking helpless as she rubbed the middle of my back. Granna and Becka even came to console me, but where was Messiah? He and Qui were nowhere to be found, which was an indication that they chose Pete and went to check on him instead. "Sue! Get your ass over here and come see about your child!" Granna fussed, and granna never cursed which was shocking. "NOW ENOUGH IS ENOUGH! YOU DON'T PAY THE CHILD NO ATTENTION BECAUSE IF YOU DID... SHE WOULDN'T BE HERE RIGHT NOW!"

"MAMA!" Becka tried to stop the argument that was brewing.

Granna stayed solid. "DON'T MAMA ME BECKA! SHUCKS, IT'S THE TRUTH!"

Sue stood over me looking like my older twin sister, that's how strong our resemblance was. I didn't like the look in her eyes because I didn't know what she was thinking at all, but if I could put my finger on it... she wanted to whoop my ass. Her nostrils flared and the entire rhythm of her breathing changed. She didn't address anything granna had previously said; the only person she was focused on in this tiny space was me and only me... like we were the only two in here. "Nah, fuck that shit... Bari tell me what you have to tell me!" She demanded.

Becka rolled her eyes and blew a hard breath from her mouth, "Oh, Sue please! Give the girl a fucking break and get over yourself... whatever Bari has to say she can say it on her own fucking time... not when you say."

"Becka, shut the fuck up... you didn't raise your own fucking child... bitch don't tell me how to raise mine!" Sue got back at her with a low blow that even had granna shocked. Sue swore she'd never throw that in Becka's face. I felt even worse cause if it wasn't for me, my little family wouldn't be falling apart.

"Now wait a damn minute!" granna squealed at her only two daughters. "You two will not act like I didn't teach you a damn thing about how to act in public! Now Sue, you apologize to your sister! Becka you do the same!"

"But mama..."

Granna cut Becka off, "No! You two apologize!"

"I'm not apologizing to her!" Sue snapped.

Bambi cleared her throat and stepped a few feet away from me, "I'm sorry. Ya'll know I love both of ya'll but I thought this was about Bari?"

Sue and Becka both grilled each other. "Bitch always thought she was better." Becka hissed. It was really weird because Sue was way closer to Ronnie than she was me, and Becka was way closer to me then she was Ronnie... it's like I should've been her child and Ronnie should've been Sue's.

"What the fuck did you just call me?!" Sue snapped and immediately went to charge in toward Becka. All hell was about to break lose and I know the people were gonna put me out and have them both locked up. In a matter of seconds the room was in frenzy as the both of them stood off in each other's face ready to go blow for blow... I had to do something. The saliva built up inside of my once cotton mouth, followed by my gagging reflexes... because from the pit of my stomach, to my throat, I felt as though I was about to vomit all over the place.

"I'M PREGNANT FROM TUFF!" I blurted. "HE'S BEEN SLEEPING WITH ME SINCE I WAS 14! HE GOT ME PREGNANT ONCE BEFORE AND NOW I'M PREGNANT AGAIN! HE KILLED RONNIE BECAUSE RONNIE FOUND OUT AND I DIDN'T DO ANYTHING ABOUT IT! I SAW IT!

I SAW IT! BUT I DIDN'T KNOW HE WAS GONNA DO THAT! I DIDN'T TELL BECAUSE I LOVED HIM!" The way the room all-of-a-sudden became silent, you could hear a pin drop in this bitch as I sobbed uncontrollably. Eight sets of eyeballs were glued to me. Bambi wasn't shocked because she knew everything. Granna had tears rolling down her eyes, the color drained from Becka's skin and Sue... well Sue wanted to fight me!

Smack! Were the sounds of her slapping the shit out of me taking me right up off of my feet followed by her landing on top of me plummeting me with non-stop blows to my face and my body. I wasn't sure where the blood was coming from, but I taste the blood inside of my mouth. Sue was a fighter so it wasn't easy to get her off of me. I couldn't even make out what everyone else in the room was saying because the ringing from my ears blocked everything. "Sueee!" I begged. "I'm sorry! Please don't kill me!" I found myself having flashbacks of the same night Messiah had attacked me but I was starting to feel like Sue was a little more vicious than he was. "YOU FUCKING BITCH! YOU GROWN ASS BITCH!" My mama cried as her warm tears land on my face while she continued to attack me. "YOU FUCKED MY MAN AND YOU LET THE NIGGA KILL MY BOY?!"

Wham! She took one hand and used it to lift me by my throat and then slammed the back of my head onto the floor. I dazed out but the pain was so unbearable that I could no longer open my eyes. "Nooo!" I heard Bambi's voice but instead of standing near me, it sounded like she was much further away. *Wham! Wham!* She slammed my head two more times.

Apparently Becka must of snapped out of it, "Sue! That's enough!"

I felt the weight of her body being lift up off of me as she wildly swung her arms catching me in the face once again. "Aiight ma! That's enough Sue! These people bout to call the police on everybody in this bitch!"

"LET ME GO GU! I'M THE FUCKING MAMA! YOU THE SON! YOU DO AS I SAY NOW LET ME THE FUCK GO!"

"Nah Sue..." I heard his reply in his smooth, calm voice. "You gone kill the girl... come on, ya'll gotta get outta here."

I scoot my way into the furthest corner in the room where I continued to sob. Again, Bambi was right there with me trying her best to wipe the blood from my mouth and wherever else. My counselor rushed to the door. "THE POLICE ARE ON THEIR WAY NOW! I SUGGEST EVERYONE LEAVES HERE... NOW AND RIGHT NOW! BARI... WOULD YOU LIKE TO PRESS CHARGES?"

I shook my head 'no'.

"DON'T WORRY! NEXT TIME I'M GONE KILL THE LIL TRAMP AND THEN SHE WILL SURELY HAVE TO PRESS CHARGES!" Sue yelled the entire way as Gu carried her out. Granna shook her head and followed behind.

Before Becka walked out, she gave me one disapproving look. "I can't believe you Bari... get yo'self together." She sneered in a low whisper before grabbing her own bag and heading out. The only two people that remained in the room was myself and Bambi before my counselor came back with a nurse to clean me up.

"We're gonna have you checked out Bari." Mrs. Reynolds kneeled down in front of me examining my face. "In the meantime, I'll be asking the facility to hold all family visits until further notice." I simply nod my head again. "I'll be right back." She rushed out as the sound of her heels echoed against the tile floors of the hallway.

"Thanks for staying with me Bambi." I thanked my best friend without actually looking at her. To keep my eyes open were very painful but I was almost sure they were both beat swollen.

"I already told you... you my dawg Bari. I'm not ever going nowhere but I'm glad that the truth is out." She sniffed trying to hold back her own tears.

I tried to ignore the feeling of throbbing in my chest, but in a crazy and ironic way, I was glad that it was over too, I really was. This was the second beating I'd survived and yet and still, my little baby bump was growing and growing. I didn't even have to hide it anymore at this point. I had to even admit to myself that after this ass whooping, I no longer wanted a baby because it would've been from Tuff. I needed this baby to keep me alive because I didn't have shit else to look forward to now. Not Pete, not Sue, Becka, granna, or Messiah. All I had was a best friend and a baby.

'A COUPLE OF WEEKS LATER'

"Mrs. Reynolds." I walked into her office and voluntarily took a seat before she even told me it was okay. She wore soft pink and rose gold today... very pretty colors, and she was always in a good spirit, but me on the other hand, I was going crazy. I couldn't receive calls, I couldn't place any and I couldn't have any visits either. It was all me and I was once again secluded from everybody, but Mrs. Reynolds said this was for the best.

She looked up from her notepad and smiled, "have a seat Bari... how are you feeling today? You're looking much better." She stated referring to my bruising.

I was still feeling a little insecure about them because my black eyes weren't swollen anymore, but you could clearly see the discoloration around my sunken eyes. Not like I needed any more damage done to me. Mrs. Reynolds even assigned a nutritionist to me to make sure that I received fattening meals and exceeded the amount of calories that I needed in order to get me back on track as far as my weight cause going from 135 to 116 was a drastic change for me. "Thank you." I smiled. "Um I was wondering, has anyone even reached out to see me at all?"

"Well... not yet, which isn't uncommon... you just need a little time to yourself." She then sat back in her chair using the tip of her pen bringing it up to her mouth as if she was in deep thought. "Bari, I know you've been doing really well in group sessions but I wanted to speak with you one on one. If you can... can you please give me an direct break down of your feeling? Anything that you're feeling about your entire situation."

"As far as what?" I asked.

"Anything."

I sighed. "It'll be much easier for you to ask me what you want and then I can just directly answer you. You can ask me anything." I assured her. One thing about it, being in those afternoon group sessions while talking to everyone else and even listening to their stories... it really helped me to open up more and re-evaluate with a clear mind because before coming to this place... I honestly had a hard time seeing the wrong in my situation. It was the group sessions that made me realize that while I was a victim, I was very much the problem as well and the first step to healing was owning up to my shit. I was glad that Mrs. Reynolds was seeing the growth in me and I was more than willing to handle up and accept my shit.

She nod her head as I watched the corners of her lips curve. "First I'd like to start with your childhood Bari. Tell me about that."

I had to gather my thoughts before answering that head on, and I needed to pinpoint exactly where in my childhood I wanted to start from. "Well..."

"Wait!" she cut me off, pulling her recorder from her drawer. "Do you mind if I record this? These are the types of things I'd also like to be able to play back for the parents in order to help them to better understand you."

I broke an instant sweat.

"Bari..." She placed her soft hand on top of mine. "At any point you decide you want me to turn it off... I will."

I nod my head agreeing and fidgeted with my fingers, I hated fucking fidgeting so I placed my hand on my baby bump for comfort. "Well my childhood isn't the most interesting. We've always lived in the hood and I never knew my father. Sue raised me and financially took care of me but she was never there. My brother Messiah never really had time for me because he was always with Ronnie, but they were both my protectors. I had a lot of free time, a lot. I remembered days I would sit on the stoop with my best friend Bambi while listening to the older girls talk about all the older guys they were dealing with and how much money they got. A lot of times I was bored with nobody paying me any mind. Aunt Becka has always been wild and granna..." I briefly stopped to think about granna. "Well, she never really came over that often but she'd call everyday. Messiah would give me money, help me with my homework, and do his best but it was different cause I was a girl and he couldn't teach me how to be a woman. I needed Sue for that."

"And do you strongly feel as though she wasn't there for you emotionally?" Mrs. Reynolds asked while she scribbled away on her notepad.

"Technically, she wasn't." I told the truth. "I remember when I turned 10 and she got a new boyfriend, Tuff was one of the good guys and even on days where Sue was in the streets, Tuff made sure that he came around to make sure we were okay. I got really comfortable and attached to him but I didn't understand my feelings because I was more attached to him in a boyfriend type of way instead of a fatherly kind of way. For instance, when I started my menstrual cycle, Sue was nowhere around but when Tuff found me in the restroom sitting in the corner scared shitless. He helped me by explaining to me what was happening with my body. He even called Sue and got no answer... after that he took me to Wally World to buy me everything I needed."

Her tiny nose formed a little wrinkle. "Wally World?" She asked confused.

"Wal-Mart." I giggled. "Mrs. Reynolds you're gonna have to get used to slang if you're gonna me working with kids like me."

She giggled herself, "continue."

"Well yeah, so he helped me out and stayed with me for the entire day until I felt better, and then he gave me some money to keep in my pocket just in case I needed anything else. After I got my cycle, my body started changing and I was getting attention from all kind of men so I would just start being friendly with them and receiving simple things like rides home from school, or a couple of dollars here and there but never no sex. Tuff caught a guy dropping me off to the apartment one day when Messiah was out of town and then he beat the man silly. He didn't want me talking to any guys at all, he would always tell me to just focus on school but he was also making me resent him for getting in the middle of my life. I'd already had Messiah trying to run my life and then there was Tuff too. In a crazy way that's what drew Tuff and I to each other, he simply didn't want me to hate him."

"And is that where the intimate relationship came into play?" She asked.

I cleared my throat, "If you don't mind Mrs. Reynolds... I rather not relive the details of how it first started, but I'd say 'yes' that played an extremely big part of it. I'm not sure how it even got that out of control but I went from knowing that it was wrong, to being forced to believe that it was right."

She continued to scribble, "and do you feel as though you were brainwashed to believe that everything was right?"

"In a way, 'yes' now that I think about it. Tuff controlled my mind and everything that I did. He slapped me once for even thinking that I was dealing with another boy and he would always tell me that one day he was gonna leave Sue and it would be him and I. We was gone run off and live a happy life."

This time she dropped her pen and looked at me with sad eyes as if she felt sorry for me. "Bari..." She sighed. "You do know that was a form of manipulation don't you sweat heart? You're a minor Bari... this fling that the two of you had went on since you were fourteen. You're gonna be seventeen in a week and you're carrying the child of your molester."

I hated those words, and as much as I tried to steer away from it, the best thing to do was to face it. "I'm aware... I never saw it then but I see it now." I admitted. "And while I should be opting for an abortion, it's a little too late for that Mrs. Reynolds. I'm five months and I'll be finding out what I have soon. I've lost my family and even Pete... this baby is gonna be my only family."

"What are your feelings for Pete?" She asked catching me off guard. I really tried not to think too much about Pete but it was hard, really hard. Pete was gonna be graduating soon and I at least wanted to be able to talk to him again. I just wanted to hug him and apologize a thousand times.

"I did Pete wrong." My throat even burned when I said it. "Like, for as long as I've known him, he was always the good guy but I played a foul game by lying to him about being pregnant for him... once again trying to cover up for Tuff and that was stupid of me."

"I understand... and I think that's very responsible for you to even acknowledge your wrongs... but may I give you a little suggestion before you go running behind Pete?" She questioned.

I shrugged, because all-of-a-sudden I didn't wanna talk no more. This was making me too emotional. "I guess."

"Well, in regards to your situation with Pete. This is the advice I'd like to give. Every relationship you go through leaves holes in your heart. But, make sure you take the time to fill yourself back up. Going from pain to pain can destroy you as well as the other person, especially when they don't deserve it. Heal before you deal and everything else will follow behind."

"You're getting deep Mrs. Reynolds... real deep, but I understand." I stood up to get ready to leave. She peeped her watch as well while rushing to grab her belongings.

"Shoot! I was supposed to meet my husband for lunch."

"No problem, I'm gonna sleep before group session tonight anyway."

She made sure she put the recorder back and then tucked her notepad inside of her workbag. "Great, and if you choose not to go to nightly sessions tonight that's fine with me. Our personal session made up for that."

"Thanks." I told her with a half smile on my face cause I was drained from even talking to her, so forget about a group session cause that was just too much.

"See you tomorrow Bari! She rushed out as I listened to the sounds of her heels echo through the hallway heading out of the door. Turning on my heels, I made it to my room and managed to avoid everybody like I'd been doing. I didn't need no new friends and didn't want anybody getting the impression that I was looking for any.

TWO

Messiah (Gu) Carter

"Where the fuck ya head been at Mayne? I'm the one fucked up round this bitch... my homey fuckin' my bitch and you wouldn't even let me 'off' the nigga." Beans said trying to get and keep my attention. Not that I wasn't listening to him or nothin' but that shit with Bari had my mind fucked up. It had been a couple of weeks since I last saw her but bein' in that facility and how all that shit played out made me really see in depth that she needed help and I was glad she was gettin' it. The shit I respected the most was how lil Pete hollered at me and still held up to his end of the bargain. I was shocked when he told me that he still wanted to pay half of her expenses to get help cause any other lil nigga or grown ass man would've folded like 'fuck that bitch and her baby' but not lil Pete though... he was a rare lil dude and we kept in contact every day.

"My bad mayne... nigga just thinkin' bout Bari." I sat on the edge of the dusty couch inside of one of the old trap spots while we waited on Cortez to arrive. "Where this nigga at?" I frowned lookin' at my watch. This shit was long overdue and after avoiding this situation, and tryna keep Beans level headed... I couldn't do it no more. It was time for these niggas to come face to face and I hope it wouldn't be a blood bath cause I loved both them niggas from the bottom of my heart on some real shit, but if Cortez fucked my bitch I'd wanna kill that nigga too cause in so many ways, it wasn't about the bitch... it was about the respect.

"The nigga ain't comin' bruh... nigga been buckin' us for the past couple of weeks." He sat down in frustration. "Let me find out you done told this nigga I'mma handle up on his ass."

That shit there didn't even move me, "you know I ain't on no sucka ass shit like that bruh... go try another weak ass nigga." I pulled my phone from my pocket to answer for Qui. "Lil mama... you okay?"

Her jolly voice blast from the other side of the phone sounding like music to my ears. She just was able to do that to a nigga. "I'm okay... I'm pulling up now, come outside."

"Aiight." I hung up and put the phone back in my pocket. I looked at Beans not knowing what he was thinking next but I needed him to sit tight. "Aye, sit tight my man... I'll be right back."

He acknowledged me with a simple nod of the head before I walked out feeling an eerie feeling in my heart. Beans wasn't gon' let this shit go. The sun kissed my face immediately when I walked out but in the same play, the cold air also smacked my face. South Florida had to be the only state with this crazy ass weather. It was sunnier than a muhfucka but dead ass cold. That's why I rocked my grey Timbs, with a matching sweat suit. My fitted cap matched my fit and my ice dripped from around my neck. I peeped lil mama sitting in her lil Q50 patiently waiting for me with Hulk sitting in the passenger side. He was a cool ass white dude but I still couldn't figure out how he let Qui drag him to all these hood ass places always looking out of place.

She smiled when she saw me and hopped out wearing a full burgundy 'Champion' fleece suit with the matching burgundy and white 'Jordan 12's'. Her hair was part down the middle and draped down each side of her face and back. As soon as I was in arms reach, she wrapped her hands around my neck allowing me to wrap mine around her waist and hug her back before kissing her soft ass lips.

"Get a room!" Hulk yelled from the passenger seat while peeking at us. When he got my attention, he waved. "Hey master!"

I threw my head up. "Sup my man." I respectfully spoke as I normally would. Didn't matter to me that he was gay. He was good to my lil mama and if she loved him then so did I. Nigga, was confident enough in myself to be around any gay nigga cause I was as solid as they came. Now on the other hand, the niggas who always was tryna clown a gay man or punk was the ones that needed to be worried about. The muhfuckas who always had somethin' to say bout them folks was the number one sign to a down low brother, or one who wasn't confident within' himself.

"Am I gonna get shot up by 2 bloods and 3 Crips around here?" He asked looking around while gripping the nape of his own shirt looking like he was clutching his pearls. "What is this place Edwards?"

We both laughed cause that shit was mad funny, but I could understand why he was so nervous. Death Row wasn't one of the most enthusiastic streets to be on. "Ain't shit gon' happen to you while I'm out here... just don't come back alone or you may be in trouble." I said answering for Qui.

"Dear Lord..." He mumbled to let the window back up and then let his seat recline all the was back no longer making himself visible in the car.

"He's so funny." Lil mama chuckled.

I looked into her sexy ass eyes and smiled my damn self. Nigga wanted her in the worst way and while it was nice building our bond based off of no sex, it was safe to say I was a man and stressed the hell out. Sooner or later, I was gon' need some ass cause now I was getting' to that point. Qui didn't have to tell me she felt the same way as well but I knew she did. The only reason I had her around here cause I needed to give her the rest of the money to pay for her books and shit and I knew if I had her waiting on me, it was probably never gone happen today. Reaching in my pocket, I pulled out a wad of money. "How much was it again?" I asked.

She cleared her throat like she was nervous and shit and I hated that cause I told her over and over, no matter what the price was for anything... I got her. Now it was different if I didn't have it then I simply didn't have it and any female would have to respect that. "It's a stack."

"Goddamn! For some books?!" I asked shocked like hell cause a nigga wasn't expecting all that. I peeled off 10 hundred-dollar bills and passed them to her. "Sheittt fuckin' paper betta be made outta gold and the lettering betta be full of diamonds. These folks done lost they fuckin' minds."

She took the money while laughing her ass off. "Thanks." She laughed so hard she snorted.

"Didn't know you turned into pigs round this bitch too." I joked.

She playfully mushed me in the head, "whatever Gu."

"But nah, forreal tho, that's how they try to fuck with us and that's why a lot of muhfuckas be quitting' college but we ain't quitting' tho so fuck that. Take the money and slap them muhfuckas in the face wit' it."

"We?" she questioned with one brow raised. "You thinking about going back to school?" she asked all excited.

I shook my head fast as hell. "Nah lil mama, I got my diploma and I'm done. That shit ain't for me but if you make it... I make it... package deal, remember?"

Her pretty smile lit up the whole block, "I remember. Well, I'ma go take care of this before it's too late and I'll see you later."

"Yeah, go ahead and do that so I can get back in here and make sure Beans ain't in there goin' crazy." I gripped a handful of her ass and kissed her again. "Make a nigga a steak or somethin' tonight... don't you think I deserve it?"

She nod her head, "you really do... I got'chu."

I opened the door for her to get back in the car and said 'bye' to her and Hulk both. I waited until they were completely off the block to go back inside and deal with Beans, I knew he was pissed cause this nigga Cortez should've been showed up. Surprisingly when I got inside, the nigga was nowhere to be found. "BEANS!" I searched the tiny house and his ass was gone. Since we always parked in the back, I opened the door to see that his car was gone too. "THE FUCK?!" I Picked up the empty mug from the table and tossed that bitch into the wall causing it to shatter everywhere. Pulling my keys outta my pocket... I hopped in my Camaro and rushed to Pembroke Pines. I knew exactly where he was going... this nigga was goin to kill Cortez ass.

I hit damn near a hunnid on the dash and prayed like hell that I didn't get pulled over on the way but I couldn't let my nigga go out like that. He couldn't have gotten too far but still. If he left as soon as I walked out then chances were he could've already been there. Hitting the horn through traffic and ignoring every phone call from my ringing phone on the way... I finally made it on his block. His car was home, but I didn't see no signs of Beans car, which left me confused. "The Fuck?" I said to myself shutting down the roaring sounds of my engine and then hopped out and banged on the door. "Yo Cortez!"

It took him about two minutes to answer the muhfucka, but when he did he was bare chest and wiping the eye crust from the corners of his eyes. "Mayne, the fuck you bangin' on the door for? You got a key..."

I push past him and searched the house. "Cause... Nigga you probably in here swimmin' around in Monica's pussy!" I fumed.

"What?" He frowned staring at me.

"You heard what I said mayne! How the fuck you round here smashin' the homey girl?"

The look in his face told it all.

"Yeah..." Beans stepped through the front door with his gun directly on Cortez causing both of us to jump." He gave off an devilish smile. "Surprise muthafucka." He used one foot and slammed the door with it.

"Damn..." I mumbled. This the shit I ain't wanna see it come to.

Cortez took a seat on the couch staring Beans right in the face. "Mayne you ain't gone kill me over no bitch, we don't even roll like that."

"Cortez!" My voice boomed through the house. "Mayne... now not the time for all that." I knew he was just as stubborn and heartless as Beans but he needed to shut the fuck up right now if it were any chances of him living through this.

"Nah." Beans chuckled. "Let the nigga say all of what he wanna say."

Cortez looked at me and tried his luck with me. I wasn't tryna see my nigga get killed and that was the truth. "Mayne Gu... my nigga we all been sharin' bitches for as long as I can remember mayne... this nigga wanna trip now?"

"Don't play stupid my nigga..." Beans pressed the barrel of his gun to Cortez head.

I sighed. "He right Cortez... you know the limits, even when it come to my bitch... you know I don't mind sharing pussy... but not that pussy. When feelings involved, that shit goes out the window mayne... handle up and speak on this shit like a man. You knew damn well Monica was off limits or you wouldn't have been moving like that on no sneaky shit in the first place."

He blew a deep breath and shook his head. "Mayne... Monica came on to me."

Beans nostrils flared and he was losing his composure. "I don't give a fuck if the bitch came over here butt ass naked with stripper heels on. She could've bent over and played with her pussy right in yo face and you should've slapped some sense into her ass and sent her right the fuck back home. Nigga wouldn't have even been mad."

Cortez sniffed knowing he fucked up. "Aiight, put the gun down nigga. Handle up man-to-man, chest-to-chest. You wanna fight this shit out lets do it."

"Nah..." Beans chuckled and cocked the gun, so quick that I

couldn't get to him in time to even stop the bullet he put through Cortez chest.

"BEANS! NOOOO!" I dived over the couch tryna get to him but it was too late. The blood oozed from Cortez chest as we both watched him gasp trying to catch his breath. "FUCK!" I felt my heart break watching my man gasping for air to save his life.

His eyes were rolling in the back of his head as he weakly pointed. "The-the..."

"The what?" My eyes followed the direction that he was pointing to, which showed a inside camera from the ceiling aimed directly on us. I nod my head and closed my eyes while whispering to him. "Let it go bruh... just let go." I looked in his eyes one more time to let him know it was okay. In order to not feel the pain, he had to stop fighting. "See you on the other side bruh... nigga love you mayne." A tear fell down my eyes. I looked up at Beans and one single tear fell down his face too. I wanted to be mad at the nigga but I couldn't cause if it were me, shit would've happened the same exact way. We both watched as he took his last breath before going to remove the tapes from the security system and walking out. Hopefully somebody found his body soon and when they did, I was ready to pay for the expenses and I knew Beans was too.

They always said deaths come in 3's and I was starting to believe that shit were true. First Ronnie, then Tuff, and now Cortez all in a matter of months and make it so bad, they all were close to me and no matter how it happened. I felt like in some kind of way, I would be wearing their blood on my chest for the rest of my life. "You aiight mayne?" I asked Beans when we made it back to the block. Night had done snuck up on us and we chilled on my stoop drinking Heinekens sad as fuck.

"Nigga... hell nah I ain't aiight mayne. That was bruh and always will be bruh. But how the fuck was I suppose to let him live with that kinda disrespect. Nigga disrespect me like that then he'll do anything ya feel me?"

"Beans, you ain't gotta convince me... I already know." I replied looking at the badass lil boys from upstairs throw water balloon at the lil girls playing hopscotch in the middle of the road. After two more Heinekens and whole blunt... I was ready to get inside the apartment but I wasn't stayin' home. I needed Qui in the worst way. "Anyway... I'm bout to head in da crib. What you gon' do about Monica?"

"I'mma let shit die down and think on that shit... but trust me, her ass ain't off the hook." He replied downing the last lil bit of his Heineken. Although he didn't say it, I knew he was more fucked up about Cortez than what he acted like.

I nod my head and just looked at him. "Yo, come on mayne, I was gone crash at Qui crib tonight but I cant let you go home all fucked up like this... come crash on the couch."

He blew a sigh of relief like he'd been waiting on me to say that shit... one thing about it, we knew each other too well. "Thanks bruh... nigga appreciate that." He stood up and tossed the bottle.

"Use the key to let yo'self in... I'mma go get Qui and let her come sleep ova here cause I need my girl tonight."

He nod his head. "I feel you."

I shot across the building to Qui crib and let myself in. As soon as I opened the door a strong stench of strawberry lemonade hit my nostrils. The apartment was dark as fuck and candles were lit all through the living room. I knew the steps of her apartment well enough to make my way to her room where I needed to be. Midway to her door I bumped into somebody head on. Boom! "Ahhhhhhhh!" The mystery person used some kind of towel or cloth whacking the shit outta me... and it stung to.

"What the fuck!" I blurted grabbing the towel tussling with whoever the fuck this was mad as fuck that I left my burner in the crib.

"It's an intruder Edwards!" Hulk yelled still swinging the rag.

"Mayne stop fuckin' hittin' me with that muhfuckin' towel!" I knocked his ass to the floor just as the hall light flicked on. Qui stood there with nothing besides her panties and bra on with a bat in her hand. If I really was an intruder, what the fuck was that gon' do? She looked funny as hell standing there in a batter stance like she was bout to knock my ass to a home run.

She squint her eyes and lowered the bat, "Gu?"

I was madder than a muhfucka as me and Hulk came to a stare down, and he had the nerve to have on a pair of tight long johns with a bare chest... couldn't believe this muhfucka had nipple rings as he brought his hands to his chest covering it. "Oh my god master!" he gasped. "Sorry, thought you were trying to rob us or something." He rushed off with a red, flushed face from embarrassment.

I grilled Qui and shook my head, "Forreal yo?"

I peep how hard she tried to muffle her laughter. "I'm sorry..." she giggled, "you know Hulk is paranoid as fuck."

"Well what he doin' here then?" I questioned walking past her to her bedroom.

Before she could answer, he was walking from the bathroom wearing the top to his Long johns and a blanket wrapped around him. "Man problems." He volunteered the information. "Like seriously, I don't understand how I could love a man so much and he not even appreciate me ya know? It's been going on 3 years and he acts as if monogamy is such a big deal." He plopped on the edge her bed while she slipped her robe on her body. I didn't say shit, I just listened.

"Awww Hulk... I told you it'll be fine, he's gonna come around and if he doesn't then move on cause there's more fish in the sea."

"I don't like fish." He sneered with his nose tooted up.

She chuckled, "well you know what I mean... all I'm saying is if he cant respect you, then move on to the next, telling him he's in the way of you seeing all the men behind him."

The fuck was she talkin' bout? "Yo lil mama... you spittin' a lil too much knowledge for me right now. Bet not be no niggas standin' behind you tho."

"It's only you baby." She smiled and winked at me.

"Ughhh." Hulk said. "Not now love birds, this is about me... you two are just sickening." He rolled his eyes and then looked at me. "So master... since she may say the wrong thing... do you have any advice you can give?"

Now, I wasn't used to havin' these conversations with gay men so I was gon' spit this knowledge and get the fuck on. "You either gon' cry about it or boss up."

"Well first of all... I'm gonna do both." He sneered.

"Well that's ya answer then..." I replied and then focused back on lil mama. "Um, when you get done getting' yo'self together... come to my apartment aiight?"

"I'm gonna sit and talk to Hulk for awhile so you might be sleep."

"Don't matter... wake me up." I stood up to leave. "Oh and if you see a body on the couch, don't get scared and start attacking muhfuckas like Hulk did me... it's just Beans."

"Humph... is everybody's bestie goin' through something tonight?" She furrowed her brows.

"Dam sho seem like it." I stated with one hand on the doorknob. "Aiight Hulk... be easy mayne.. and stop all that weak ass cryin'. Charge that shit to the game and start over wit' somebody bigger and better." I let him know watching him wipe the tears from his eyes. After the door slammed behind me, I used my key to lock up and ran back to my apartment. By the time I got back inside... Beans was on the couch knocked out with all his clothes on just like a real hood nigga. Dead ass sleep with his shoes still on and fully dressed; gun on his waist with one hand in his pants. Same hand he was gon' try to dab me up with tomorrow and he had me fucked up... I was gon' remember that.

I hit the shower and got under my blankets with nothing besides my boxers on and just like I knew... my mind was gone drift off to Cortez and the last look he gave me. Even in all his pain, he still wanted me to get the tapes outta his house just so we didn't get caught. Tomorrow I was gonna burn them shits. I shook that shit outta my mind the best I could and rolled over falling asleep. I don't know what time it was when Qui walked in but I smelled the vanilla rub down on her body before I even felt her presence. I pulled her in my strong arms and pulled her on top of me allowing her to straddle me. I already knew she'd taken off whatever she had on before she even got in the bed with me cause she had a habit of sleeping in her panties and bra or with nothing on at all. It had been one long ass week and I needed one of those hugs that turned into sex.

"You okay?" She asked with her head on my chest.

I told her the truth. "No."

"What's wrong bae?" She asked kissing the tip of my chin. The lights didn't have to be on for me to see her eyes and know that she genuinely cared.

"Qui... I need you, like a nigga really need you now, and I hope you ready but if you not then I understand."

Her body didn't tense up or nothing like I expected her to; instead she brought her soft lips up to mine and kissed me allowing me to gently suck on her tongue while cupping both of her ass cheeks giving her a better feel of what she was doin' to a nigga as she woke my monster up. Crazy part was, there wasn't shit to talk about, all we needed was to follow the strong connection between us both. I was aware that she was a virgin and I was gonna have to be gentle with her; I was gone try my best not to tear that ass up.

For the first time, I really had a chance to explore her body and appreciate her curves while I licked on her neck and earlobe feeling the moisture from her pussy raining down on my shaft. "Put it in Gu..." She moaned with a soft whisper to my ear that made a nigga instantly get brick hard. The only other virgin I'd ever fucked was Nessy and I learned from her that it was easier to just let them sit on top and sit on the dick at their own discretion since only they knew how much pain they could take. "You sure?' I gripped her ass and licked on a shoulder blade. I felt her nod her head 'yes'. With that confirmation, I used one hand and grabbed a condom out of the top dresser drawer of my nightstand before ripping it open. "Pull it out and slide it on lil mama." She grabbed it from my hand and adjusted herself so she could do just that. Her hands felt so fuckin' good sliding down my dick rolling the condom on and when she did, she lift herself to match the height of my dick in order to sit on it. I gripped her hips to help her and to make her feel a little more comfortable letting her know that I was going through this process with her.

She got real tense when it was time to sit on the dick but with me guiding her it made it easier. I was aware that I was bigger than average and in her mind, she was probably thinking I was gone rip her shit in half. I felt the tip of my dick on her warm opening as she took her time to sit inch by inch. "Ssssss." She winced in a lil pain and came back up. I took charge and rolled her from off top of me onto her back. "I'm sorry." She said quietly.

"Don't be... I got you." I used her hands and intertwined them with mine holding them above her head while I licked and sucked on her neck on down to her nipples and worked my way down. This was a new feeling for her and I was aware, especially the was she squirmed trying to control her breathing.

"Ouuuuu... ssssssss." She moaned and whimpered in pleasure while my tongue found its way down the middle of her stomach to her freshly shaved pussy. I was quite impressed with the thickness of it cause it was nothing worse than fucking a skinny ass pussy; nigga wanted to actually feel like he was fucking a grown ass woman and not a child. I used the flat more softer surface of my tongue and gently licked on her clitoris before going to work on the whole pussy. Every time she tried to run, I spread her legs further and held them back allowing my tongue to vibrate. "OH MY GODDDDD!" she gasped bucking her pussy in my face. She had a nigga so hard, I felt the pre-cum oozing in the condom. She used her nails to dig so deep in the skin on my shoulders a nigga wanted to scream but I took that shit like a 'G'. "I think I'm about to cum!" She squealed not sure of what exactly it was she was feeling but when I felt the clit swell up and get a lil harder... I knew what time it was and just to make her orgasm a lil more pleasurable... I put my tongue on the spot right above the clit and licked back and forth. "Ahhhhhh.... Ohhh shittt!"

Her legs trembled like butterflies; I knew she was ready now cause that pussy was fountain wet.

In one swift motion, I rolled over and sat her back on top of me. This time when she inched her way down it was a little easier as I felt her tight pussy walls grip my thick meat. A nigga was in pure heaven feeling tight walls and warm, wet pussy. "Oh shit!" I closed my eyes and gripped her hips showing her how to ride the dick like a pro. She was slow at first working through her pain and I could tell. "It's gon' feel good in a minute baby." I reached up and kissed her lips.

Instead of responding, she tried not to focus on the pain until her body enjoyed the pleasure in it. The moment she was comfortable and feeling the dick, I knew it cause her body moved way differently than before as she rocked her hips back and forth meeting my motions. "Ouuuuu Gu! Its feel so gooodd!" She placed her hands on my chest and rode the dick like a pro. I smacked her eyes and tried my best not to scream out like a lil bitch cause Beans wasn't gon' ever let me live that shit there down. I was gon let Qui enjoy tonight cause after she was officially broken it; I was gone be tearing that ass up. We went on like two dogs in heat and both erupted at the same exact time. She instantly fell on top of me mixing our warm seat and fluids with each other.

She was breathing hard as hell but I understood. I placed another soft kiss on her lips. "You okay?" I asked her.

"Um hmm." Was all she said before she fell asleep with my dick still in the pussy. In the middle of the night, I managed to roll her off of me so I could go move the condom and flush it and then take a piss. When I came back out, Qui was sitting up naked in the bed.

"Don't move... I got you." I rushed back in the bathroom to get a warm rag and then applied just a dab of witch hazel on it. I gently cleaned her up down there with my dick still dangling. Even on soft, my shit was still big... nigga was blessed.

She shook her head just staring at it. "I cant believe I let you put that thing inside of me. Did I bleed?"

I looked at the white rag and showed it to her. "A little."

She smiled. "You know I love you right?"

"You know I love you too right?" I leaned over and kissed her lips. "Ready for round two?" I asked.

"Un un." She furrowed her brows. "I'm sore as hell... I'm gonna need a few days."

"Days?" I frowned.

Boom! Boom! Boom! Somebody knocked on the door hard as fuck.

Qui clenched the sheets to her body giving me a 'what the fuck' look probably thinking it was a bitch. I grabbed my gun off the dresser and slipped on a pair of basketball shorts. "Wait here." I told her.

"Yo Gu!" Beans yelled from the other side of the door unaware that Qui was still in here. I looked at the clock 5:45 a.m.? The fuck?

I barely left a crack in the door not wanting to expose Qui's naked ass under my sheets when I walked out. "What's up mayne? The fuck is that?"

"It's ya Bm." He whispered not wanting to alarm Qui.

"Mayne the fuck she doin' here?" I frowned and went to the door with Beans right behind me. Snatching the door open, she stood there with no Winter with her so what the fuck could she possibly want. "What?"

She stormed her way inside with tears in her eyes while pacing back and forth. "Cortez is dead!" She yelled grilling us both. "Monica just called me having a fucking fit! You two can't tell me ya'll ain't know!"

"The fuck would she be having a fit over him for?" Beans frowned.

Nessy knew that she was about to slip and give details of some shit we were already aware of. It was her and Monica's dumb asses who thought they were a quarter slick, but we already knew what time it was. She dropped her eyes. "I don't know... she just... man ion know shit! Ask her, not me! Point is that's ya'll homey and he's dead!" She snapped, especially when she wasn't getting the reaction outta us that she would have liked to get. "Oh my God!" she threw her hands up over her mouth and studied Beans. "You knew didn't you?" She walked up on him.

"Knew what?" He questioned. "Yo Gu... get ya baby mama mayne."

I stepped around him and confronted Nessy, "yo you way outta line Hennessy, especially bout some shit that ain't got nothin' to do with you... take ya ass home mayne... we'll handle everything else."

She shook her head, "ya'll ain't shit forreal."

It took everything in me not to back hand her talking ass. She had me fucked up and the only reason I ain't show my ass was cause Qui was still in the back room probably clinging on to every word she heard out here. "Go home." I warned again with my nostrils flared while grinding my back teeth really tryin' not to snap.

She was now more focused on me and tooted her nose up. "You smell like a female been all over yo ass Gu, like straight vanillas. And look at that fucking passion mark on yo neck... is a bitch in there?!" She yelled.

I grabbed her arm and snatched her ass up. "Get the fuck out! If you even think you gon' disrespect my shorty you got me fucked up mayne!"

Beans stayed out the way and looked from the hallway to the front door making sure Qui didn't come out the room. Nessy went crazy! "Do she know that you still love me! I can have yo ass if I wanted you! SHE KNOW YOU GOT A BABY ON THE WAY FROM THAT BITCH RARA?! HUH GU?! DID YOU TELL THE BITCH THAT I JUST GOT LOCKED UP FOR YOUR ASS CAUSE I HAD TO FUCK THAT BITCH UP!"

Damn! I knew it was no way Qui didn't here all that shit. I seriously didn't wanna put my hands on the girl but I damn sho didn't have a problem with tossin' her ass out the door like a bird. I didn't give no fucks... baby mama or not! You acted like a bird then you get treated like a fucking bird... period! She hit the floor and looked up at me with daggers. "Fuck you Gu!"

"Nah... you mad cause you can't. This shit here ain't even about

Beans... it's only partial. You act like a nigga owe you somethin' like you caught a charge for me or some shit with that dumb ass girl. I bond you out and got you a good ass lawyer to get that shit off ya record. Nigga been tryna be nice to you ever since but if you ain't throwin' pussy... you throwin' attitude and I can never fuck with that. So, once again... get the fuck outta my presence... go call Monica and gossip like always... bye mayne." I slammed the door in her face. She knew not to knock again, she used all my patience for the next 48 hours... just a pure fuckin' headache.

I turned around to see Beans sitting on the couch looking off into space. "I cant believe Monica really fucked up bout that nigga... what, she loved him?" I could see the hurt all in his eyes.

"That's a question you gotta ask Monica bruh... but if she has some kind of feeling that you did it, she might be a problem."

He sighed, "yeah you right... I'ma handle it, soon as I'm able to find her muhfuckin' ass."

"Aiight." I walked to the room and was shocked to see Qui fully dressed slipping her shoes back on with a disturbed look on her face. I already knew what the problem was. "Where you goin'?" I closed the door and locked it.

She wouldn't even look at me, "Home." She mumbled.

I tucked my gun and sat on the edge of the bed. "Let me explain."

"She rolled her eyes, "EXPLAIN WHAT!?" She snapped shocking the fuck outta me cause on God... Qui ain't never used that tone with me.

"Watch yo tone lil mama... I'm respecting you, respect me."

"Boy... fuck you." She hissed.

"Okay... I'ma let you have that pass... just that one but don't ever try me like that again lil mama." I took a deep breath and tried to keep it together. "Qui, a nigga don't got no baby on the way first of all, the bitch is lying."

"So you mean to tell me ya baby mother lying Gu?!" She asked sarcastically.

I shook my head, "No... but the bitch who said it is lying tho." I told her in all honestly.

"Humph that's funny... somebody just wanted to pin a baby on you huh?"

I shrugged, "don't act like it ain't possible... shit like that happens everyday. Shit, you watch Maury."

"Haha... real funny."

"Your baby mother just went to jail for you? What the fuck is up with that?" She asked. All the while she was still talking and gathering her shit that she had at my house.

"Listen, RaRa came to my baby mother on some real foul shit and Nessy beat her ass... that's why Nessy got locked up, she ain't did shit or no favors for me like she tried to make it. She's the one that beat the red off of RaRa's head. Did I bond her out... yes. Did I pay for her lawyer... yes. But that's it mayne. I'm not fuckin' the girl and definitely don't want her. She only said that shit cause you was up in here. Now that's the truth."

All she did was shake her head. "It's really sad that men play these kind of games Gu."

I stood up from the bed and frowned cause she was getting a nigga pressed like a muhfucka. "Look! How many times I gotta tell you a nigga ain't lyin' huh? I speak four different languages... which one you want? No estoy mintiendo! Mi nuh lying! Mwen pa bay manti! Je ne mens pas!" I broke that shit down in Spanish, patwa, creole, and French! The fuck did she want from a nigga!

The look on her face was everything, but she was too stubborn right now to address a side of me she hadn't known shit about yet. "I've seen this girl."

"Who?"

"The RaRa girl... your baby mother."

The fuck was she talking about? "First off that ain't my baby mama, and second... what the hell you talkin' bout?"

"She came to my job a lil while ago. She was brown skin with strawberry colored hair that was styled in a short cut. She hated me no matter how nice I was to her and the entire time, she rubbed on her belly."

Now this was the kind of shit that I didn't play. Okay, so she addressing Nessy is one thing... but to show up on my shorty's job was somethin' totally different. "Qui look... was I fuckin' the girl? Yes, but that was way before I met you and she was cut off before I met you too. I recently got a petition to take some DNA test like around the time that Tuff died. Did I sneak off and take the DNA test? Yes I did cause I'm sure that baby ain't mine and I don't give a fuck what the hood say. I strapped up and was careful every single time."

She looked at me sideways. "What did the results say Gu?"

I shrugged, "shit ion know why the shit takin' so long but I'm still waitin'."

She pierced her lips together. "Okay... cool." She grabbed her house keys and tried to walk past me. I wasn't goin' for that shit. I grabbed her gently by the arm. "Qui, don't do this." A nigga damn near begged.

She looked away from me. "You know what's crazy? It's not even that you may potentially have a baby on the way. It's the fact that you hid it. Package deal remember? I thought we didn't hide shit from each other. If we start building on lies now... it'll always be built on lies Gu."

I sighed and felt a slight stab to the heart cause she was right, "I fucked up... the only reason I didn't say shit was cause I didn't wanna disturb our relationship with the shit being that I'm positive it ain't mine."

"Yeah... but you still should've told me."

"You right, and I can't even argue that. I apologize Qui."

She snatched her arm away. "Okay... but I'm still going home." She walked out. This time, I didn't even follow her. I was aware that I probably needed to give her some time to cool off and that's it. I damn sho wasn't givin' her a lot of it either... she had me fucked up.

THREE

Messiah (Gu) Carter

THE FUNERAL WAS PACKED JUST like we knew it would be. My nigga Cortez brought the city out... even niggas we hadn't seen since the sandbox were in the building at this funeral. Now, while most of the niggas were genuine... it was a lot of niggas dressed in their best just tryna cop hoes anyway cause that's what they did. Everybody knew there was 3 places that you could for sure bag some new bitches and that was the club, a funeral, and church on Sunday's. It sounded fucked up, but it was true. We went all out for the homey too requesting that everybody wear black since he was buried in royal blue, his favorite colors. His casket was royal blue and chrome as well as his flower arrangements. Only other people that were permitted to wear that color was the homey's and that's it.

CORTEZ and me stood off to the side strapped cause seemed like funerals were another place where niggas with some kind of fake ass beef got cocky and wanted to act up, but I was here to let a nigga know first hand... I'll bust his muhfuckin' ass. The preacher was talking but I font think Beans or me heard shit he was sayin' cause it fucked both of us up to see Cortez in the casket but I had to come to terms with myself that no matter how much I loved the nigga, he was a snake and snakes belonged in the ground. Nigga cross you bout some pussy, he'll cross you about anything. The Saint Laurent shades that were pulled down over our eyes disguised the tears that burned our red eyes. I had to get high as fuck to even come to this shit cause only the Lord knew I almost didn't make it. I tried to convince Qui to come with me but she was still mad at a nigga and she had to go to her counseling session too. Speaking of her being angry, when she got back today, I was about to put a end to all this beef she had goin' on with me, even if I had to break her fuckin neck cause a nigga ain't did shit to her ass.

AS FAR AS RaRa's trifling ass, all I needed was to see some results to prove the world wrong cause while I may have been on some killer shit any other time, I wasn't about to kill no pregnant bitch or her unborn child. Nigga wasn't that cold, fuck that. "Yo, you aiight mayne?" I turned my attention to Beans as his eyes focused on a lady tryna console Ms. Loretta, Cortez mama... damn.

"YEAH MAYNE... I'M AIIGHT." He nod his head and looked on through the service. When the pastor asked anyone if they wanted to speak up and say some kind words or final goodbyes on the behalf of Cortez, a few people got, including all the hoes he was fucking and all. But what really caught our attention was the last man that stood up to speak. "The fuck is he doin' here bruh?" Beans furrowed his brows.

I EXAMINED the older cat wondering if I'd seen him anywhere and I can't say I could ever remember seeing dude. "We got some beef, he the other side? Nigga what? Let me know." I prepared myself to handle up any way that I may have needed to cause a nigga like me was trained to go.

"NAH, that's the nigga that my mama say is my daddy... triflin' ass nigga was on drugs back in the day and ain't wanna have shit to do with my lil ass."

I EXAMINED the dude and he was damn sho right, Beans did look just like his ass. However, he didn't look like he was on drugs no more. He looked as healthy and fresh as any one of us niggas up in here GQ as fuck. "Ion know..." I shrugged, "shit I guess we bout to find out."

We watched intensely as he grabbed the microphone and looked long and hard at the open casket before he let a tear fall. "You know... I never got a chance to meet my son, but I never thought that it would take this circumstance to do so." He sniffed. "I'm not ashamed to admit that my drug addiction played a major role in me missing out on Cortez life, or any of my boys lives for that matter. From what I hear, he was a pretty decent young man and I'll always live with regret knowing that I didn't get a chance to formally meet my boy... I- I just- I..." before he could get the rest out his knees buckled and he broke down.

I LOOKED over to Beans to see if he was okay, this was some fucked up shit. The only piece of him that I caught was the back of his suit making his way out the door. I couldn't even imagine how he must've felt knowing that he killed his own brother. I don't know why nobody ever put two and two together in the first place cause them niggas did look alike. I didn't wanna make a scene so I didn't yell his name to stop him, I just casually made my way out the door but when I reached outside, something was wrong, something was very wrong. The Miami police had the fuckin' church surrounded and Beans stood there with a regretful look in his eyes. "PUT YOUR HANDS IN THE AIR!" One of the officers yelled pointing his gun at him. Beans did as he was told.

"YO what the fuck goin on?! Ya'll do realize this a fuckin' funeral right?! The fuck wrong with you pigs!" I fumed.

"BACK UP!" Another officer warned me.

"MAN SUCK all the inches of my dick bitch!" I spat and backed away a little.

BEANS LOOKED at me and gave me a stern look. "You know they look for reasons to shoot us mayne... chill bruh, I'll be aiight." He said tryna remain strong. I watched helplessly as one of the officers slowly made their way to him and placed his arms behind his back and then slapped the cuffs on him. "Cordell Maxwell, you are under arrest for the murder of Cortez Dukes. You have the right to remain silent. If you do say anything, what you say can be used against you in the court of law. You have the right to consult with a lawyer and have that lawyer present during any questioning. If you cannot afford a lawyer, one will be appointed to you if you so desire."

"HE CAN AFFORD A FUCKIN' lawyer!" I yelled. "Yo Beans, I'm on top of it mayne! Stay strong! Don't fold mayne, just stay strong!" I assured him wondering how the fuck they were able to pin point him in anything. There was one person and only one person who could've possibly had something to do with this shit and that was that trifling bitch Monica. I knew Nessy's trifling ass wouldn't give up her where-abouts but if it was the last thing I did, I was gonna find that bitch. She had me fucked up. I knew for a fact that she had a nice account set up that Beans dropped money in for her on the regular. Knowing that slut bucket, she probably ran outta state somewhere but she must not have known who the fuck I was. She was gone pay, I already lost one brother behind her ass and I wasn't about to lose two. By the time he was in the back of the car, Mrs. Loretta was at the door with a crowd full of people behind her asking me what was going on. I couldn't even look her in her face, instead, I made my way to my car and bounced. I was on yet another mission.

IRONICALLY AT THIS moment I didn't want nothin' or nobody but my girl. I sped to my apartment and rushed to change clothes but to my surprise... Qui was there cleaning up for me looking all cute in her lingerie, she was the only person that I knew who did that kind of shit but I liked it.

"GU!" She gasped jumping when I burst through the door, "shit! You scared me!"

"QUI!" I rushed to her and broke the fuck down. A nigga literally broke down on my knees and placed my face up against her soft stomach just so it can catch my tears. She didn't say anything, instead she embraced me and got down on her knees with me placing tiny kisses all over my face. When I looked up, she was crying too. "What's wrong baby?" She asked concerned.

"YO, I don't even know what the fuck no more lil mama... just promise me one thing." I stared at her on some look me in the eyes type of shit.

SHE PALMED my face with her hands and stared back at me intensely. "Talk to me Gu."

"YO, you the only person that make some kind of sense in my life right now baby, promise me you gon' always remain solid. Don't switch up on a nigga and if shit get rough, don't bail out on me aiight? Promise me that lil mama... I love you mayne. Nigga can't do this shit without you, just be my backbone cause every nigga need a spine."

SHE KISSED my lips and nod her head, "Gu, I love you more than anything and I promise."

I NOD my head and stood up helping her up as well and then I embraced her in a tight hug. "Good... thank you baby."

SHE LOOKED up in my eyes again. "Tell me what's wrong?"

I SHOOK MY HEAD, "trust me when I tell you some shit is better left unsaid and I promise to always tell you what you NEED to know."

"I UNDERSTAND." She whispered.

THERE WAS a knock on the door that distracted us both from our thoughts. "I got it." I got myself together and walked to the door. It was the mail lady with certified mail for me.

"THANKS." She smiled when I signed my signature before she walked off.

"WHAT IS IT?" Qui asked by the worrisome look on my face. Not that I really had anything to be worried about but still, I just didn't like the feeling of having to deal with this shit. I passed the letter to Qui. "Here... you open it."

I DIDN'T EVEN HAVE to tell her what it was for her to know, she slowly ripped it open and read the results. I couldn't quite make out the look on her face but I just wanted to see her smile knowing that the baby wasn't mine. Instead, she did the opposite and her eyes dropped. "You are the father." She said in almost a whisper.

MY HEART DROPPED! I walked over to her and read over the results to make sure she wasn't misreading the shit. "Ain't no fucking way!" I snapped and grabbed my keys. "I'll be back!" I rushed out the door... I wasn't even surprised when Qui didn't try to stop me, I only prayed like hell she was still there when I got back.

FOUR

Rayliris (RaRa) Almanzar

I STARED down at my DNA test results from ear to ear cause I just knew that Gu thought my damn test was gonna come back negative. All those hoes in the hood was talking about me talking bout I didn't know who my baby daddy was all cause Gu kept denying paternity of my child. One thing about it, if I got the results back then so did he and I knew for sure that he was gonna be happy once he overcame his anger, especially if I gave him a boy. "What you smilin' about Ra?" Swain walked in the living room all in my business as usual. Before the results came knocking on the door, I was all balled up on the couch engrossed in Love and Hip hop Atlanta while eating a tub of butter pecan ice cream and enjoying the precious kicks from my baby. I passed him the paper so he can read it for himself.

A HUGE SMILE spread across his face but at the same time, I could tell he still wasn't pleased that I was pregnant from somebody other than him, which was crazy cause I never even fucked him and didn't want to. "Here..." he passed it back to me. "That's wussup... now what?"

I SHRUGGED, and got off the couch to go get dressed and go to my aunt's house before heading to go and get my school uniforms since she washed them for me. I wanted to be all set for classes on Monday. I'd been going to school for the past month and I loved it. At first I was going in hopes of getting Gu's attention so he could actually see that I was really trying to do better. "I'm going to my aunt's house right now and then after that I'm going to get me something to eat."

"YOU KNOW WHAT I MEANT... what you gon' do about dude?"

"OH... I'm gonna try to make my family work." I replied in all honesty.

HE SUCKED his teeth and stood up to leave as well, "You silly as fuck." He snapped. "How the fuck you gonna make some shit work with a nigga that wont even claim the baby? You need to get yo shit together." He grabbed his key and slammed the door.

TRICIA CAME from the back with a robe on and her hair wrapped since she'd just hopped out of the shower from washing it. "What the fuck is his problem now?" She frowned.

"GIRL I DON'T KNOW." I chuckled. "That's yo man girl... yours!"

SHE SIGHED, "whatever girl... seems like since you've been pregnant he's been trippin' and it's really fuckin' with me cause I know he wants a child."

I WATCHED the uncomfortable look in her eyes like something was bothering her. "Un un what is it?"

"I THINK Swain might be cheating on me." She confessed her worries.

I FELL out laughing cause that shit was mad funny, Swain wasn't cheating on her ass. "You joking right?" She didn't laugh with me; I stopped laughing. "Oh shit, you serious?"

SILENCE.

"COME on Tricia don't shut me out now."

"GIRL IT'S PROBABLY NOTHING." She said trying to disregard it my questions.

"NO... fuck no! what did he do? We'll fuck his ass up!" I fumed. Now I know he played his lil petty ass games with me but I wasn't going for him cheating on my friend, the fuck was wrong with him?

"CALM DOWN... maybe it's nothing but he's been leaving a lot lately and not answering when I call. On top of that all types of weird numbers have been calling my phone and as soon as I answer, they hang up."

"DEFINITELY A BITCH..." I mumbled while nibbling on my bottom lip, another pregnancy habit. I tapped my nails on the counter thinking about how we could catch his ass.

"RARA!" she snapped me out of my thoughts.

"WHAT!" I frowned.

"STOP TAPPING yo nails so hard girl... before you break one, and trust me when you do... I'm not filling them for you."

I SIGHED and grabbed my purse. "Sorry girl... but we'll figure it out. Let me go to my aunt's house to get my uniforms for class on Monday." I wobbled toward the door. "I'll be back." I said closing the door behind me. I made my way to the parking lot and hopped in the little 2014 Nissan Altima that Swain had purchased for me from the auction. It was three years old but it still was in excellent shape and only had one previous owner. It was getting more difficult to sit in the car and even put my seatbelt on without being uncomfortable.

"AUNTIE!" I made my way up to her door listening out for her or one of my brothers, which were never around but when nobody came to the door, I used my key to walk inside. I was glad to see that she left my uniforms out on the couch for me and I appreciated that. It wasn't that I didn't love my aunt cause I did, especially since she's the one that raised me; we just couldn't live together cause we clashed a lot. She wanted me do more with my life then what I was doing, but I just wanted her to let me live my life and figure this shit out. My mama died while giving birth to me. After my two brothers Raymond and Rondo... the doctors warned my mama that she should tie her tubes and not have any more kids due to her heart condition. When she got pregnant with me, she was informed to have an abortion but her love for me wouldn't allow her too. She died in order to give me life and it fucked with me every single day, that's why I didn't like to even think about her cause it made me sad. It was hard as fuck not growing up with a mama around and leave it to my brother's, they would've turned me into a real damn tom boy out here since they wanted me to be a boy so bad.

WHEN I TOLD them about my pregnancy they were both a lil iffy about how they felt about it, especially since they probably wouldn't be around to help since we weren't close like that. Besides, they told me they'd probably be moving away to Tampa before the baby was even born, which was fine by me. I still had a little time to kill and didn't wanna go back to Tricia's place right now so I opted to make me a ham and cheese sandwich with some miracle whip spread on the bread; that was my favorite. I turned the radio on to 103.5 the beat and listened to Charlemagne talk shit before they played some Beyoncé. Turning the music up, I danced around wit my belly in tow while munching on my sandwich.

SORRY I AIN'T SORRY, Sorry I ain't sorry, Sorry I ain't sorry. Middle fingers up, put them hands high, wave it in his face, tell him boy bye, boy bye, middle fingers up, I ain't thinkin' bout you. Let's *have a toast to the good life. Suicide before you see this tear fall down my eyes. Me and my baby we gone be alright, we gone have a good life.*

I MUST'VE DANCED myself around that entire living room cause that's exactly how I felt, I mean sure I wanted Gu to be here for me, and I wanted to be a family with him but if he didn't wanna accept it then fuck it... at least he gave me something I could cherish the rest of my life. I knew he was probably still pissed about me popping up on his baby mama and picking a fight with her but I was sick of that bitch. She needed to understand that she wasn't the only one. Hell, I was still debating about pressing charges or not and if he didn't want me to press charges on his daughter's mother than he better had made his way to at least talk to me about our child. I had yet to find out the sex of the baby and I didn't wanna know because I wanted it to be a secret. I wouldn't be having any gender reveals or nothing in that nature. When I popped he or she out, that's when I'd know if we were having a boy or a girl.

AFTER ABOUT ANOTHER 30 minutes of scrolling social media and just fucking off time, I decided that it was time to go so I grabbed all of my things and wobbled my way out the door making sure to lock it back. I pushed the button to unlock the trunk so I could place my uniforms in there and I wasn't surprised to be greeted my Meka walking down the steps. I wasn't feeling her ass cause I kind of felt as though she still had a thing for Gu. Meka was fucking him before me, before we became friends and when I started fucking him... all of a sudden she wanted to befriend me and everything was bestie this and bestie that. I thought she was cool and all but I didn't like the shit that I was hearing about her tryna jump on the niggas dick every chance she got; although he turned her around every time it was the principle of the matter.

"HEY GIRL." She spoke. "When yo baby shower?" She questioned.

THIS BITCH WAS TOO SLICK for me, plus she was the hood gossip. "Why?" I frowned. "You ain't invited... only my peoples, my baby father and his family."

SHE GAVE OFF A LIGHT SMIRK, "His family huh? Girl... he don't even claim that baby."

I WAS ABOUT to put an end to al the hood gossip right at this moment and what better way to do it than with Meka's talking ass. I dug down into my bag and pulled out the results from our paternity. "Well he'll be claiming my baby now." I teased tickled by the shock on her face. I knew she'd go around and tell everybody...to hell with her.

SHE READ the results and gave me another fake smile before she said anything else. Matter fact, I didn't even wanna hear shit else she had to say so I placed it back I my bag. "Well congrats to the both of ya'll." She said, I knew she didn't mean that shit, but whatever.

"THANKS..." I said dryly and walked to the driver side of the car and tossed my bah on the seat. Although it was hot, my car was still cool cause of the dark ass tints that covered my windows. When I looked out the rearview mirror, Meka was gone walking back up the stoop to her apartment... good! I crank the car up and was all prepared to pull of but what I didn't expect was to feel a pair of hands wrap around my mouth from the backseat. "Ahh...!!!" I tried to yell but was cut off. A lump formed in my throat and tears instantly burned my eyes.

From the rearview mirror, I could see Gu's eyes. The same eyes that used to look at me with so much love, now looked at me with so much hatred.

"BITCH!" he growled placing the gun up to the side of my head. I wished somebody could've helped me, but with these dark ass tints I knew there was no way that anybody could see what was going on in this car. "I'ma give you a couple of seconds to explain to me how the fuck you pulled this shit off or I'mma blow ya muhfuckin' head off."

I BREATHED AS SLOWLY as I could and not so deep because his hand was cutting off my breathing. I nod my head agreeing as I felt my tears sliding down my face and landing on his big warm hand. He removed his hand but not the gun. "Gu-Gu..." my lips trembled. "I don't know how it happened." I cried. "Maybe the condom bust or something Gu... I don't knowww!"

HE YANKED me hard by my short curls giving me a feeling of my neck snapping. When I heard the 'pop' I thought I was gonna die. "Ahhh!" it hurt so bad.

HE BROUGHT his lips up to the side of my ear as his beard hairs tickled my neck. "Bitch! I'mma try this shit one more fuckin' time RaRa! You think I'm stupid yo?! If that were the case then why everybody knew you was pregnant besides me then huh? Why the fuck you change ya number and play all these games and shit? Cause any bitch pregnant from Gu and wasn't on no snake shit woulda been happy for me to share this shit with them yo! I was mad careful and I always strapped up... nigga didn't want no baby from yo ass, or nobody else for that matter!"

HE STILL HAD me by my hair and it was starting to hurt my neck but it was time to address this shit head on. "Nobody besides Nessy right?" I blinked the tears out.

"NESSY AIN'T GOT shit to do with this bitch! Now how the fuck you trick me into bein' ya baby daddy?!"

I GASPED for air cause the way he was holding my neck was cutting my circulation and if I wanted to live to raise my baby then I'd better start talking. "Ok! I did it okay!" I cried. "I poked the holes in the condom that night we came back from 'The Mint' you were drunk as fuck and when you went to the bathroom... I did it!"

I DIDN'T EVEN HAVE to look at his face to know he had a look of disgust. "You gotta be the most dumbest and trifling bitch I know, not to mention desperate as fuck!"

"I WANTED A BABY GU."

"WELL BITCH! That ain't the way to go about it! You go have a baby from a nigga who wanna share that shit with yo ass!"

"BUT GU...."

HE REMOVED THE GUN, "Nah hoe! Don't 'but Gu' me bitch.

This what you gon' do... you gonna stay the fuck away from my baby mama, and you gon stay the fuck away from my girl. If I hear any different I swear when you drop that load... bitch I'll put you six feet under." He spat.

THAT SHIT HURT, "What about the baby Gu?" I wiped my eyes.

HE STROKED his goatee and flared his nostrils. "As much as I wanna say fuck you and that baby... I'ma just say fuck you, forreal yo. From the bottom of my heart, fuck you Ra. I hope you don't think this baby gone change shit cause a nigga ain't bout to be wit'cho ass straight up so you can cancel all the fairytale ass family shit going on in yo sick ass head. Next time I hear from you, it better be after the baby is here." He got out of my car and slammed the door so hard that my passenger window on the driver's side shattered, even with the tints.

ALL I COULD DO WAS cry and soak in my misery. Like why couldn't he see how much I loved him? I loved him so much that I was willing to go through all of this trouble and he still didn't love me back. I prayed I had a boy cause I needed something to turn this around. I had about four more months left and I knew that I had to remain stress free and humble. Most of all, I had to stay the fuck out of everybody's way.

FIVE

Turquoise (Qui) Carter

IT TOOK me three whole months and a lot of prayer to be standing in front of this building but I made it. After doing sessions with only myself and my parents; I had yet to face Rain but now was the day and I was more than ready. "How are you feeling Edwards?" Hulk ask me as I cradled the phone in between my ear and my shoulder in order to adjust my pants before walking in.

"I'M FINE I GUESS... I just wished I didn't have to do this alone."

"WHEN DOES MASTER COME BACK?" He asked.

"HE SHOULD BE BACK some time this week. I'm not sure why he suddenly had to go to North Carolina but it's probably business."

"SPARE ME THE DETAILS HUNNY... I don't want to get locked up for being an accessory to anything."

"OH TRUST ME... ME EITHER." I mumbled, "that's why I didn't ask and he already made it very clear that he would only tell me what I needed to know." I mumbled.

"UNDERSTANDABLE."

"OTHER THAN THAT, we're fine and going stronger than ever, he's trying to get Beans back home and that's been stressing him."

"AND THE BABY?" He asked.

"HE DOESN'T SPEAK much on it but I know whenever that child is born he's gonna be a standup guy." I replied really not wanting to think about the trifling ass girl. When Gu allowed me to listen to the recording on his phone of his confrontation with her...I was beyond shocked and disgusted that women would even take those extreme measures just to try to trap a man.

"HMMM." He hummed. "And I'm assuming that our bottle of Hennessy has been on her meds lately."

I FELL OUT LAUGHING, a good laugh too cause I needed that. "You so stupiddddd." I cracked up.

"I MEAN, it's very true dawling." He said in his gayest tone.

A HUGE SMILE spread across my face, "Little Winter is adorable though, and she loves me. Gu has to keep Nessy in check to make sure she doesn't try to play games but to my knowledge... he's still gonna file for visitation because he doesn't wanna deal with the bull-shit for the rest of his life..." I explained looking down at my watch. "Shit! I gotta go! I call you back!" I rushed and hung up the phone. Taking a deep breath, I walked inside wearing nothing but confi-dence. A few months ago, I would've still be too weak to see Rain but today... I felt nothing. I wore the heart of a Lion. She no longer had power over me to try and ruin my life.

ALL EYES WERE GLUED to me when I walked in the office but instead of sitting by anyone. I opted to sit alone. My mother sat there looking less stressed but worried because this was her first time seeing Rain since my party, and my dad's too. Rain on the other hand, she looked smoked the fuck out, like all she did was sit in the house and smoke weed all day long. She hated me and I could still see it in her eyes. The therapist walked in next, a nice lady, Ms. Richards and I loved her because our one on one sessions are what helped me to cope and learn about forgiveness. She smiled and took her seat behind her desk. "Good afternoon." She smiled. "I apologize for running a little behind. The lunch traffic was crazy."

WE ALL GAVE her a smile and nod our heads. I felt like if I didn't say anything to Rain, that I was gonna vomit. "Rain... I forgive you!" I blurted.

EVERYONE'S HEAD snapped in my direction. "Not right now Qui, just wait baby." My mama gave me a reassuring look.

"NO..." I said casually. "I forgive her and I want her to know. Are you even gonna look at me Rain?"

"FOR WHAT!" She snapped. "Look at you for what Qui?"

I SQUINT my eyes. "you still hate me huh?"

"AREN'T YOU GONNA STOP THEM?" My daddy asked Ms. Richards.

SHE SIMPLY SHOOK HER HEAD 'NO' and continued to watch. "In a minute, they need to get this steam off their chest now. This will help me to understand the underlying issue here."

"BITCH I'LL ALWAYS HATE YOU." She grilled me.

"BUT WHY?"

"HOW MANY TIMES I GOTTA TELL YOU IT AIN'T ALL

ABOUT YOU?! LIKE, LIFE DOESN'T REVOVLE AROUND QUI! WHO THE FUCK ARE YOU!"

"I NEVER ACTED LIKE THAT RAIN! THE FUCK?! I ALWAYS TRIED TO MAKE YOU LOVE ME, EVEN AFTER YOU DID ALL THAT EVIL SHIT TO ME!"

SHE ROLLED HER EYES, "YEAH WHATEVER."

"YA'LL GOTTA STOP THIS." My daddy intervened.

"NO!" She snapped. "You the problem too! The both of ya'll you and mama! Ya'll always made me feel like I wasn't good enough!"

MY MAMA STOOD up in her chair. "That's not true and you know it's not! You got just as much shit that Qui got if not more! So your selfish ways are all on you!"

IT WAS Rain's turn to stand up. "Lies! You never treated me as good as you did Qui! I bet if I was your biological child you would have!"

"NOW THAT'S JUST CRAZY RAIN!" I snapped. "You are her biological child you idiot! The weed has surely made you crazy!"

"I FOUND my birth certificate long ago! No the fuck I'm not!"

MY MAMA DIDN'T DENY that, like why the fuck wasn't she denying it. Why was she standing there crying like her heart had been broken? It was my daddy's time to stand up. "I think it's only fair that I be the one to address this and not my wife because it's not her fault."

"HAVE A SEAT." Ms. Richards ordered calmly. "I need everyone back in their respectable chairs."

WE DID as we were told but I still wanted to know what the fuck Rain was talking about.

"RICKY..." Ms. Richards said. "Please... explain."

HE SAT down with a look of hurt and regret in his eyes as he revisit a place that he obviously didn't want to. My mama reached over and grabbed his hand. "It's okay baby. I forgave you long ago so there's no need to beat yourself up about this."

HE NOD his head and cleared his throat. "Rain is right about what she's saying... when I was younger and still trying to live a fast life. I cheated on my wife with Rain's mother."

"WHAT?!!" Rain and I both blurted unexcitingly.

"IT'S TRUE." He sighed. "My wife left me after that but only for a short time and after about six months of counseling and therapy she took me back. Rain's mama was just a fling I met in a club one night and she was a real party girl. She didn't want a baby so I took on that responsibility with the help of my wife right by my side." He then gave my mama a soft smile. "I'll forever be grateful to her for that because she didn't have to raise Rain as her own child, especially when infidelity was involved."

"AND WHERE IS Rain's mother now?" Ms. Richards asked.

"THE LAST I HEARD, she overdosed and died a couple of years back but I never wanted Rain to know about this. My only concern was her having a good life and growing up in a good home. I had no idea that she would find that birth certificate before we got a chance to fully explain to her." He then looked at Rain. "You hate the wrong person baby girl... if you wanna hate somebody then hate me cause Qui did nothing to you."

"NO! She was always treated better and you know it! No matter how much you tried to ignore it!"

"THAT'S NOT TRUE RAIN." I took up for my daddy cause while this situation was fucked up, she wasn't being honest. Rain only saw what she wanted to see.

SHE CONTINUED TO SCOLD HIM. "Nah! Every time I did something wrong everything was taken away from me! Everything! And it was her fault!"

HE SHOOK his head and disagreed with her. "Rain just stop it! Every time you were punished it was never her! It was me... I did that even when she tried to fight for you!"

I COULD TELL that really got to Rain cause even from across the room, I saw he swallow the lump in her throat. "It was you?" She squint her eyes.

HE NOD HIS HEAD, "yes... it was me! She only did what I asked her to do as my wife! So you're acting out toward the wrong people baby girl." He lowered his tone a little. "You hate your own sister because she has her biological mother? Your mama didn't want you Rain, and I had a woman good enough that put her own feelings of hurt and betrayal to the side in order to help me raise you. After that, she then gave me another child and I had to beg her to do that because she felt like you were only two years old and you needed more time with her before a new baby came... so you see... you don't understand."

I HAD tears coming down my eyes and so did everyone else, even Ms. Richards as she allowed us to air out our skeletons. "It don't change how I feel..." Rain said. "Even when it came to my boyfriend. Butta loved me." She cried. "He loved me so much but then he got close to Qui too and everything I did was wrong!"

I HAD to defend myself now. "He loved me as a lil sister Rain! And he treated me better than you ever did! When he was around, he didn't allow you to do wrong to me and you hated it! That didn't mean he wanted me! I was glad to actually have him around cause he cared and you didn't!"

AN EVIL GLARE appeared on her face as she looked at the three of us with so much hatred. "Yeah, well I guess that's why I had to kill his ass... it was either gone be me or my lil sister and he couldn't have both." She said in a tone so cold I felt the chills coming up my arms. This bitch was crazy.

"WAIT---WHA- WHAT?" My daddy choked up looking in the eyes of his oldest child. My mama couldn't say shit, just gasped.

MY HANDS FLEW to my mouth, "Rain..." I dropped my eyes and shook my head.

SHE LOOKED TO MS. RICHARDS. "Can you get dispatch on the line and have them send an officer out please? I'd like to confess to a murder."

"SHE DOESN'T KNOW what she's saying!" My mama looked at Ms. Richards with pleading eyes and then to Rain. "Please! Stop Rain!"

RAIN DIDN'T REPLY, she looked at Ms. Richards and nod her head. Since Ms. Richards was now in shock. Rain picked up her own phone and dialed 911. "Yes, I need an officer to come out to 2992 West Dixie Highway please. Yes, it's an emergency, I'd like to confess to a murder." She hung up and smiled, but again, not a normal smile. She was psychotic as fuck. "I'll be waiting outside. I rather rot in jail than to have anything else to do with you lying muhfuckas." She sniffed and walked out.

I DIDN'T KNOW what to do, and neither did my parents as we both seek comfort in one another indulging in a group hug while Ms. Richards rushed out behind Rain. This had to be one of the hardest days of my life, I swear it was and it hadn't even been a full 24 hours. I had to come to terms with myself that Rain was never gonna like or accept me for her own selfish reasons, it didn't matter what they told her... I'd always be a problem, which meant I'd always have to watch my back when it came to her and that sucked because she was my only sister. "I love you guys." I cried and told both my parents.

WHEN WE WALKED out of the building, Rain was already being hauled off and refused to look back at any of us. There were no words that could express what either of us were feeling but Rain was poison. I didn't have a problem with my parents; we had a good relationship and even the time that I stayed away from them after my party, I missed them. I didn't stay away because of them, I stayed away because of Rain hoping that if I stayed out of sight out of mind then she would feel a little differently about them but obviously nothing was gonna work or change that. It wasn't even a need to get a lawyer or anything for her since I'm sure their wouldn't be a trial since she clearly and openly was ready to confess to murdering the love of her young life.

IT ALL MADE good damn sense now why Butta's mama didn't like Rain; mama knows best, but damn. When the news aired about finding Butta's body in an abandoned home like a robbery gone wrong; I would've never thought that my own sister was the one that put a bullet in his head... all because she thought that he wanted me; her arch enemy. This was sickening. "I just wanna go home." I mumbled hugging both my parents again. Neither one of them wanted me to go home and be alone, but it was best. After promising them that I'd call as soon as I got there; they let me go so I could ball up under my covers and sob in peace. I knew they were about to hit Rain with some serious time but even still... I would still make sure she had money on her books and send her holiday cards, even if she didn't accept it because that's just the kind of heart I had.

WHEN I FINALLY DID MAKE IT home, I showered and put on a simple pair of tights with a sports bra. I then took my hoodie and placed it over my head and then threw on a pair of tube socks. It was getting dark out and my stomach was growling but I didn't have the energy to even get up and cook anything so I ordered a pizza from Papa Johns since Pizza Hut would no longer deliver in our area cause the bad ass lil boys kept robbing them. The minute you would call them and give the address, they would hang up on you quick. I looked at the time and sighed thinking about Gu. I missed my man but I couldn't stay up all night and wait for him to call cause I had work in the morning and then class right after. After about thirty minutes of laying there, I got up to go and pay for my cheese pizza and then closed the door behind me and sat it on the counter so I could pull a paper plate from the counter and a can soda from the fridge... judge ya mami; I hated washing dishes.

AS SOON AS I finished my first slice, I raced to the room to catch the call on my phone before I missed it thinking that it was Gu but when I looked on the screen, it was a number I didn't recognize. "Hello?"

"UM... IS THIS QUI?" The females voice asked.

"WHO IS THIS?" I questioned.

SHE WASN'T ALL-RUDE when she spoke, she actually had a nice calm tone. "This is RaRa... I don't mean to be bothersome but I'm in labor and I cant get Gu on the phone. By any chance, is he with you?" She asked.

THIS BITCH HAD some real nerve; I didn't even know how the fuck she got my number, but I wasn't gonna let her even think she got up under my skin. "Well I'm sorry to hear that but Gu isn't here... try again." I hung up. Since I didn't know what he went out of town for, I wasn't even gonna volunteer that information to her ass. Oh fucking well.

AFTER BEING with Gu all this time, I knew for sure that RaRa trapped his ass cause he was super careful not to slip, even with me and I knew he loved the shit outta me. I was low key pissed as fuck and then all of a sudden there were the feelings and the thoughts that this nigga was actually having a baby and it wasn't with me. I hated it! It made me sick to my stomach knowing that he was gonna have to be around this baby and the mother. I hoped that he didn't fall weak and allow this child to get him in trouble or blind him. Even with tears in my eyes, I still put my selfishness regarding the situation to the side and picked up the phone to call him and let him know that his child was about to be born. He didn't answer for me either so I shot him a text and went to sleep to prepare for the day ahead of me. No need to stay up and make myself sick by dwelling on the situation.

SIX

Messiah (Gu) Carter

'Bitch I rock a chain like a field nigga, how the fuck you real and you squeal nigga, roll that pressure up and pop a seal nigga, come here baby girl I'm tryna build with ya, heard you gettin' money how it feel nigga, she pulled up with a real one how it feel baby, bitch I rock a chain like a field nigga, how the fuck you real and you squeal nigga.'

I bopped my head and vibe to my nigga Money Man 'How it feel' in these cold ass North Carolina streets following this bitch Monica around all day long. Luckily I was in a lil low-key bucket that my homey Paul let me borrow while I was out here. Instead of booking a flight, I drove cause I didn't wanna have shit linked to me, and when I got here, I didn't wanna have a rental linked to me either so I parked my car in Paul's garage and hopped in his lil bucket. Besides, I didn't need Monica to know I was anywhere in town and that car of mine was a dead giveaway.

She was so clueless to what was going on that she probably wouldn't have noticed me anyway as she rode around in a brand new baby beamer with the tricked out rims. This bitch was in and out of stores all day long spending the money that my nigga Beans had been droppin' on her ass and she had me fucked up. Now my bruh was sittin' behind bars all cause a slimy bitch got in her feelins' and decided to hop on some dick she had no business lookin' at in the first place' bitch shouldn't have even been able to sniff the dick. She was the only person who could've even turned the police on to Beans and if she thought she was gon' show up in court and do her thang on my homey she could forget it. She should've known that a nigga like me wasn't even going for no flake ass shit like that.

It was cold as fuck today and plus I needed to get back home. On top of that my phone was blowing up and I ignored that shit; no calls would be answered cause I couldn't risk fucking up. I sat in the parking lot of Saks waiting for Monica to come back out but after about two hours I realized the bitch wasn't coming out no time soon. It was a good thing that I manipulated her back door while she was in her big ass house last night. I don't know how she thought that she was gonna hide and nobody not find her but I was one persistent ass nigga and if I wanted it, I got it. I made my way back to her house but I parked the bucket on a side street and then hopped her gate to get inside the back door of the home.

She had this bitch laid out too. Placing my gloves on my hand, I made my way to the fridge and helped myself to a glass of fruit punch while rumbling through all the healthy food she had in the fridge and I didn't want none of that shit. I chose to sit on the couch and spark me a joint while letting the darkness surround me. Since I was dressed in all black, it would be hard for her to even know that I was sitting here. In a matter of 20 minutes, I'd smoke two fat ass joints until I saw the headlights from her car pulling in the driveway and then inside of the garage. I listened to the sound of her driver door slamming and then the sounds of the chirping that came from the side door of the garage letting me know she was making her way inside as she to maneuvered through the dark sitting the bags down on her living room floor.

After a dew more seconds, she turned the light on and picked up a handful of mail shuffling through it with a unit on her face. When she slammed it down and looked up this time... I was still in the same spot on the couch with my gun aimed in her direction. "Shit!" her arms flew up to her chest.

"Don't run bitch." I growled. "Don't even fuckin' think about it. Sit down." I nod my head once in the direction of her love seat so she could sit down and listen. From the look in her eyes, she knew shit was over for her. I didn't have much time to waste sitting here having a lil night cap with her and neither did I have time to waste by sitting here asking questions or staring cause she knew what time it was. "You shoulda chose a different set of friends to try to come in and fuck with Monica... you fucked up with this one baby girl."

She squint her eyes and wiped her tears, "how did you find me?" She asked trying to get herself back together as if she was accepting her fate or some shit.

"It doesn't even matter... I thought you was the smart one at one point but I guess I shoulda known better. You got my homey fucked up.

"I didn't do shit to him!" She yelled.

Boom!

My gun sent one right in between her eyeballs in the middle of her head. She died on impact and a nigga didn't give a fuck. I stood up to leave out the back door but the chirping from the side door was distracting me, somebody was coming. "Baby!" Some nigga rushed to her side, some nigga who she was probably already fucking. His lame ass sobbed over her body until I put one in his ass too sending him to go be with the trifling bitch. After that, I was satisfied but tired. The cold wind smacked my face as I made my way to the bucket and pulled off like I was never there. I stopped to get me some food and then made my way back to Paul's house since I wasn't checkin' into no hotel or no shit like that, besides, I just needed a couple of hours of sleep before I hit the road.

"You good mayne?" Paul asked walking out as I was walking in.

he had a bad lil shorty on his side too, which made me miss my own shorty even more.

"I'm good." I nod my head. I'mma take a quick nap and then I'm out.

"Aiight bruh... well... I'll probably be gone all night so just lock up and I'ma fuck with ya'll boys when I come down on that side aiight."

"Bet." I gave him a brotherly hug cause it was definitely all love.

I must've slept for about a good three or four hours and when I woke up, I finally checked my phone. I had multiple missed calls from RaRa and Qui both so I called Qui back first. "Lil mama..." I said when she answered in her sleepy voice.

"I miss you Gu." She yawned. "I got a lot to tell you when you get back."

"I miss you too baby."

"RaRa called me." She sighed. "She's in labor."

I furrowed my brows, this was the shit I was talking about right here. "I told that bitch to stay away from you."

"Technically she has, she called me, not found her way to my presence."

"Yeah... aiight."

"Are you gonna go?" She asked.

"I'm still thinkin' about it."

"Gu..."

"Yeah?" I asked agitated mad all over again that this bitch done trapped a nigga with a baby.

"I know you hate her, but don't make the baby suffer."

"I hear you." I mumbled. "But look, go back to sleep aiight? I'm on my way back."

"I love you." She sang in my ear.

"Love you too."

'THE NEXT DAY'

Every step I took in the hospital was a step closer to me strangling RaRa's little ass neck. I didn't know how her labor went or what she had and if she thought I was gonna be in that delivery room holding her hand and consoling her, she had me fucked up. I wasn't tryna give her the illusion or no hope... period! Matter fact, I didn't even wanna see her. I stopped to the nurse's station. "Good afternoon. Rayliris Almanzar is on this floor, she recently gave birth."

"And how can I help you?" The bright eyes nurse stared in my face and smiled.

"I'm the child's father. Messiah Carter, you can call her and confirm that if you need to."

She held her hand up as if a light went off. "Oh yes! One second, I know exactly who you are and she's reserved a parent band for you so you can come into the hospital to see the baby any time you'd like.... Here you go." She wrapped the blue hospital band around my wrist, which was an indication that I had a son. As tough as my ass was I felt a tingle in my heart; I had to see him to believe it. "Would you like to see Rayliris? She's probably in there resting."

I shook my head, "I rather not... but I would like to see my son if that's okay."

"Sure." She walked around the desk to lead me to the nursery. "He's such a handsome little baby with a head full of hair."

That was good to hear.

"And how much he weigh?"

She turned her nose up in deep thought and then pierced her lips. "I wanna say he was 7'7 but don't quote me on that." I nod my head understanding how hard it must have been trying to remember the weights of every baby born on the floor. "That's him... the one right there with the badge that says Almanzar." She led me inside; babies now surrounded us. I couldn't lie, a nigga was in awe. "Would you like to hold him? Wash your hands first." She ordered not waiting to get an answer as she rushed to wash her hands to and then picked my lil man up all bundled in his lil blanket sleeping peacefully while all the other babies were fussing.

She passed him to me and I immediately fell in love, no lie. I hated his mama, but I loved him with everything in me. "Hey lil man." I looked in the face of my lil twin, it was no denying that he looked exactly like my baby pictures. "What she name him?" I asked the nurse.

She picked up the chart and read it, "Um let's see... we have Messiah Carter Jr. here on the clipboard."

While I wished my junior could've been from somebody that I actually wanted a kid from... I was still happy that he was a junior and a part of my legacy would be left behind when I was dead and gone. I was so happy and in love with him that I Face timed Sue, granna, Becka, and Qui so they could see him. I hadn't even been fuckin with Sue them like that but since we were big on family, I knew they'd still be happy either way, no matter how MJ got here... since that was the name that I'd given him already.

I sat with him all day while his mama slept. I even got a chance to change him, feed him, and burp him. He was cool while he was with me but every time one of the nurses came in to run some kind of test or some shit, that's when he started cutting up and I didn't like to hear him crying; they was bout to piss me off. "Shhh it's okay lil man, daddy got you." I put the pacifier in his mouth and rocked him back to sleep. When I looked up, RaRa was standing in the door way looking a fucking mess with her hospital gown on. We locked eyes and spoke an unspoken communication. What was understood didn't need to be explained, I was gonna do my part but I wasn't fuckin' with her ass at all.

Since she was there, I decided it was time for me to go so I placed him back inside of the little bassinet that they had assigned for him. I wanted to kiss his little face but I knew little babies were real sensitive to germs. Looking at him one last time, I walked out and stopped in front of RaRa going inside of my pocket. I peeled off a stack off of my money roll and placed it in her hand. "Understand, this is for him... not you, cause a nigga ain't takin' care of yo ass."

She grabbed the money, "Gu... don't leave." She said with tears in her eyes.

I didn't give a fuck about her tears. "I had a beautiful day with my son... and that's all this shit about yo. Text me the address where you gone be stayin at so I can send some stuff over there. And don't think you gone be on no bitter shit like Nessy thinkin' you gone keep my baby away from me cause ya'll got me fucked up. I'm filing for visitation rights on both of mine, I'ma do this shit through the courts before I end up killin' one of ya'll... I'm done playin' with you muhfuckas... period."

"You ain't gotta do all that Gu, I wasn't gon' do that anyway." She said softly. I didn't know who she was tryna fool with this nice girl shit but she must've forgot, she was the same bitch that trapped me and if she'll do that, she'll do anything.

"Yeah, well I am... period. You did all this and we still ain't about to be a family now you and Nessy both gon' watch me go be happy with somebody else... somebody who actually got some damn sense."

"Yeah.. aiight Gu." She replied all hurt.

I turned to walk away and realized it was one more thing I forgot to tell her so I quickly turned around. "And another thing... don't hit my line if it ain't about the little one cause we ain't friends and we don't got shit to talk about."

She rolled her eyes and slowly walked over to our son, it was her turn to spend some one on one time with him. I walked out the hospital feeling differently than I'd felt walking in, cause after seeing his face... he was the only person that made me feel better. Now I had to explain to Winter that she had a lil brother before Nessy did it in a evil ass way. Everybody knew she did that kind of shit.

By the time I made it back to 'Da Nolia' everybody was congratulating me and shit on my new bundle of joy. It was crazy how news spread like wildfire around this bitch. For months I'd been hearing about the lil bickering about my family, Bari, this baby and everything else but nobody was crazy enough to address me or even ask me about it. "Heard that girl had a baby." Bambi rushed down the step designer down with some flowers and a card in her hand.

"Yeah... she did, it's all good though. Where you goin'?" I frowned.

She eyeballed the flowers, "Oh... the facility granted Bari visitation again. She's doin' real good too and she even looks like herself again. She sent me some pics." She smiled. "I'm about to go see her real quick."

"Is that right?" I stroked my goatee wondering if Sue them was aware of this. "And the baby?" I asked.

"Oh, it's a boy and her home schooling through the facility is goin' good to... in order to make sure she didn't stay behind, they set that up for her. They said once the baby is born she can't stay though. But that's cool cause she'll be more than ready to go."

I had to admit, that was good to hear. "Who you goin' with?" I asked her.

"Pete gonna meet me there."

"Pete?" I asked shocked. "I thought he was away at college?" Pete had graduated a few months back and just like he'd been sayin' he was gonna do, he bounced, to my knowledge he had a new girl and all. I knew he was still communicating with Bari but I wasn't expecting him to wanna see her."

"What's the look?" Bambi asked. "He loves the girl, that's all."

"Yeah we all do... but still."

She looked at her watch. "Well, I gotta go. I'ma tell her you said hi and you love her!" She ran off leaving a nigga standing there. Bambi had a way of brightening anybody's mood. I didn't know how she dealt with her own situation and stayed in good spirits and tried to be there for everybody else but she was gone be blessed one day and if I ever got rich, I was gon' look out for her first quarter cause she deserved it, she was a true hustler, and she never complained about shit."

I knew Qui was at my house waiting on me and knowing her she probably had a whole meal prepared for a nigga. When I turned the key in the lock... I was surprised to see Qui and Hulk sitting on the floor playing some kind of board game with Winter. I was always happy to see my daughter but I couldn't help but wonder what she was doing here, especially with Qui. Nessy would never. "Dad-dyyyy!" Winter hopped in my arms embracing me in a hug. I kissed all over her face.

"Hey daddy baby!" I spun her around. "Who brought you here?" I asked her.

"My mommy." She smiled. "And she packed me a lot of clothes too."

I furrowed my brows, "Clothes?" I asked.

Qui cleared her throat and stood up. "Winter..." she came and grabbed her hand. "Why don't you finish playing the game with Hulk while I talk to your daddy okay?"

She smiled and agreed.

"Yeah." Hulked igged her on. "I'm gonna win this time." He said in a playful voice.

The two of them sat there and finished out the board game while Qui led me to the back room and closed the door. "What the fuck Qui?" I asked.

She threw her arms over her chest and shrugged. "I don't know Gu. She got a whiff of your new baby boy and just snapped I guess. I came here from work early and I was gonna change and then nap before class but as soon as I walked in Winter was at the door with a bag of clothes in her hand.

"Where the fuck was Nessy?" I asked.

"I don't know... I looked but I didn't see her so I brought Winter inside and she gave me this note. Of course since she can't read she wasn't aware of what it said."

I was confused as fuck right now. I was convinced somebody had they nuts crossed on me cause I couldn't catch a fuckin' break for nothin'. "Where is it?"

She grabbed it from the dresser and passed it to me. "Here."

I unfold it and read it aloud: *'Since you and yo bitch wanna be playing like ya'll this big happy family then tell that hoe to get on her step mama duties. And I heard you had a bouncing baby boy now explain to your child why she gotta share yo time and her profits. I'm heading out of town to identify Monica's body and have her cremated since I was the only family she had, but I'm sure you don't know about that either right? Bye Gu.'*

I balled the letter up and tossed that bitch trying my hardest not to get myself that worked up. I was about to lose it and Qui saw it. "Gu!" she called out to me and placed her hand on my shoulder. One look in her eyes and I felt myself calming down. "We gon' get through this okay? We will... it'll get better one day."

I loved that she kept her mind in a good place but not even she deserved this shit. Man if God could've sold me a future I swear shit would've went different. That's why they always say watch who you have these fuckin' kids from. Nigga be thinkin' bout a nut and not fully developing the consequences after. Now don't get me wrong, it really was some nigga out here who deserved that shit, but not me cause I was always a solid and stand up kinda dude. I pulled Qui onto my lap and kissed her long and hard. "I'm sorry bout this shit lil mama."

"It ain't yo fault..." She rest her head on my shoulder as we both just sat there in deep thought. I needed to get up and go pay everybody's rent but that shit was gon have to wait till the morning cause I was stressed in the worst way. Rolling Qui onto the bed, I did the only thing that made me feel better, made love to the only woman that had my heart.

SEVEN

Belcalis (Bari) Carter

'Count on me through thick and thin, a friendship that will never end, when you are weak I will be strong, helping you to carry on, call on me, I will be there, don't be afraid, please believe me when I say, count on me'

"Ahhhhh!" Bambi and me squealed when we finally saw each other probably waking up the entire damn facility. We hugged and jumped around like we hadn't seen each other in years! I missed her so much and she looked damn good as usual.

"Bitchhhh! Look at youuuu!" Bambi cried real tears. "Yo I'm happy as fuck Bari! You look sooo good! You look happy!"

I looked myself over in the mirror and was happy about my appearance too. It took a lot of work but I felt healthy again. "Thanks Friend." I gushed.

She started singing and snapping her fingers. "Cause my bestfran finna, she finna ohhhhhh...."

"Go best fran that's my best fran!" We chanted along together now. "You so emotional Bambi." I giggled.

"Girllll you my only damn friend! Of course I'm emotional." She fanned her eyes.

"Thanks for the flowers." I smiled, "and the card, that was nice too."

"You know I got you." She sat on my bed. "How you feel Bari?"

Lately I'd been a big emotional water bag, especially with the pregnancy so I wasn't surprised when the tears came. "Oh my Godddd." I sniffed. "It's been hard ya know? Real hard."

"Don't cry Bari." She said with sad eyes.

I nod my head agreeing, "yeah you're right. It's just that everything I knew as the truth was a lie ya know. I hate Tuff, I really do and I hate the fact that I betrayed my family in the process. A lot of times sitting in this place, I wish I could trade places with Ronnie and give him back his life but I know I can't do that and it kills me every day."

"You gotta push through and move forward Bari... just keep pushing. Ronnie is in a much better place now and I'm sure he forgives you."

"And what about Pete? He hates me doesn't he? Last I spoke to you about him, you told me he left for school and was dating some new girl." I said feeling sad all over again.

"Well, that's pretty much what happened but it doesn't change the fact that both he and Pete still covered all of your expenses since you've been here. And if I'm not mistaken... didn't he have you a gift sent here on you birthday?"

I smiled, "He did, with a nice card... he brought me something simple. It was a little Pandora bracelet with a charm that represents healing." I lift my arm so she could see the bracelet on my wrist. "See." I showed her.

"That was nice of him." She smiled. "I was a little tight around that time cause shit was slow but you know I got you when you get up outta here girl."

"I know." I smiled. "It was hard spending my birthday alone

though. Nobody could have told me I'd bring seventeen years in with no family by my side, that was definitely a first."

"Did they do anything here for you?" She asked.

I nod my head, "Yeah, they did a lil something. My counselor got me a nice cake and they cooked a special meal in the kitchen. It was real cool, and nice of them, I appreciated it but I missed my family."

"I know you did..." She replied. "I saw Sue and Becka the other day, looks like they finally made up. Have you spoke to them?" She asked.

I shook my head, "Sue... nah... but Becka writes me and she said that when I come home me and my baby can live with her. I think she just kinda wants to do right by me and the baby like on some second chance type shit cause she didn't do that with Ronnie. She even offered to keep him for me while I take up some college courses."

"And what about granna?"

I thought about granna and smiled. "Yo, on the real granna prayed for me daily. She was actually the only person they allowed me to speak with and every morning on the hour she called and we did morning prayer. I don't think I could've made it these few months without granna."

"That's what up Bari... you better keep that close to your heart cause most people got a family that ain't really family and don't give a fuck bout'em."

"So true..." I replied and I saw that first hand being around most of the people here and listening to their sad stories.

"Let's walk out back to the garden and sit out there, girl this room is making me depressed." Bambi suggested, but in reality, her ass just couldn't sit down in one place long enough and she'd always been like that. "It's so nice out here." She said as we sat out on the lawn chairs.

My mind drifted back off to Pete, "So what else has Pete been up to? Have you even seen him?"

She chuckled and looked at me, "Girl why you keep asking me about Pete? You realize that you're in love with that boy right?"

"Whatever," I turned my head away from her cause she was reading me too well.

"Well ask him yourself what he's been up to."

"Come on... don't even do that Bambi, you know that boy is not coming to see me."

"How you know?" The voice of a male boomed from the same door we'd just walked out of. My eyes had to be playing trick on me. "Pete?"

As soon as he smiled with those mouth full of Gold teeth, I took off running in his direction, well not really running cause my stomach was big as hell but jogging until I was directly in front of him wrapping my arms around him! "Pete! I'm sooo sorry." I cried softly, I hated what I did to him, especially when he didn't try to do shit besides help me and that was the realist shit he could've ever done.

"Mayne stop cryin' Bacardi." He joked and hugged me back making sure not to get too close to my stomach. "I forgave you a while ago, you should know I ain't even that type of nigga... you known me half yo life."

"I know Pete... but still." I wiped my eyes and grabbed his hand. "Come... come sit down." I led him to the lawn chairs.

"What they do Bam?" He leaned down and kissed her on the cheek.

"Hey Pete." She hugged him back. "It took you long enough to come, shit I thought I was gonna be answering questions about you all day." She joked but put me on the spot at the same time. I could've killed her.

"Yeah, got caught up... my fault, shit I just landed this morning mayne... what you want me to do?"

"Did you tell that fine ass roommate of yours what I said?" She questioned.

I felt so out of the loop listening to them talk making me realize how much of my true teenage life I'd missed out on worrying about being grown with Tuff. "Yeah, I did but crazy thing is... he had already asked me about you from the last visit."

"Where did you end up going to school at Pete?" I questioned.

"UCLA.." He replied.

"CALI?!" I blurted, I wasn't expecting that and I knew for sure I'd never have a chance with him now.

"Yep." He nod not obvious to my true feelings, "shit nice too.. ain't nothin' like that Cali weather."

"Well when he stops being scary, he can call me." Bambi cut us off to continue with her conversation. "Wait what?! You mean to tell me you're actually into somebody?" I quizzed. That wasn't like Bambi.

"No Bari, on some real shit you gonna have to see this nigga. He's originally from Dallas so that's what everybody calls him but he's fine as hell too. Pete brought him down here with him a couple of weeks ago and then I started seeing him all over Instagram and falling in love with every pic. Don't trip cause he like me too though. He so fine, when I graduate this year, I'm following his ass... yep, UCLA here I come cause he WILL NOT forget about me cause of some Cali bitches." She shook her head. "I'ma be all in that nigga chest." She fell out laughing and so did Pete and me.

"Wait hold on now, what's wrong with Cali girls? Shit I got one." Pete said still laughing.

My heart dropped but I couldn't let it show on the outside, I refused to let it show. Just from the look in Pete's eyes, I knew he still loved me but if he didn't wanna acknowledge his true feelings then neither would I.

"I didn't day nothing was wrong with them Pete... all I said was Dallas wasn't gone forget about me cause of them, shit. He could have his fun now but I was about to shut shit down in a minute."

"Mayne! You crazy as all hell Bambi." Pete laughed.

I played it off and laughed too as if I was actually enjoying this conversation, but in reality I wasn't. For the rest of the day I decided to put my feelings to the side and just enjoy the company of two people that I genuinely loved and when it was time for them to go, I was sad all over again. Pete didn't even act the least bit uncomfortable around my belly but the whole time he kept asking me if I was okay, or if I needed anything like I was a handicap.

Meanwhile, I wanted to be a normal teen and go attend the party that he and Bambi and probably the rest of the hood was about to be attending. After I hugged Bambi, she waited in the car while Pete spoke with me. "I wanna tank you for everything Pete... seriously."

He looked at me with that sexy face and bright eyes. Still the same Pete with a mean swag and every time I saw him his dress code got better and better. "You know it's all love Bari... I keep tellin' you that but I wish you woulda did right by a nigga from the beginning ya know? Shit still fucks with me but I can't hold no grudge forever mayne. I don't know what it is about you but a the better part of you still got a nigga heart."

I swallowed hard and nod my head, "I understand."

"Well look, I'm about to be out aiight. I'll make sure I try to see you before I go back. Make sure you call me if you need anything." He back peddled his way away from like he always did.

"I will!" I yelled once he was inside the Hummer truck. I continued to wave until I no longer saw the lights. This shit sucked, it really sucked. If I had one wish and one wish only, this shit would go way differently. I'd bring Tuff back just so I could be the one to gun his ass down my damn self. I prayed hard though as I walked back to my room. I prayed that one day peace would be upon my family again and we could get over everything. That was the plan but who knew? Only God. When I made it to my bed, I really wanted to call Messiah, especially after Bambi gave me the news that he had a baby from that girl RaRa and I would've never ever guessed that. However, my heart did smile knowing that I was an auntie again.

MY SLEEP WAS mad uncomfortable as I tossed and turned still thinking about Pete and his new girl. I'd been feeling kind of down ever since his visit a couple of days ago and I was depressed that he left for school and never made it back. I spoke to Bambi everyday and she even showed up the day before for the baby shower the facility had for me. I had to admit that I had the best counselor in this place and she genuinely cared for me. The hardest part was gonna be leaving her most of all but earlier today I got notice that my treatment here was complete and I was free to go before my baby arrived. Maybe that was another thing that I was nervous about; in the morning, aunt Becka was gonna be picking me up and this would be the first time I actually saw her since she witnessed Sue beat my ass.

I was most of all embarrassed that I was going back to the hood in fear that everyone knew my business or were going to be looking at me crazy and I honestly didn't know how to deal with that part of the bargain. I knew it didn't have to answer to nobody, but still, the shit was still embarrassing cause I didn't know how much they really knew. And then there was Messiah, I was gonna be seeing him again too and Sue... well I'm glad she'd do the best to avoid me at any cost and definitely didn't wanna have nothing to do with no baby at all, which was something I was gonna have to live with.

The morning came too soon and for most of he morning, I drug my feet around packing up with the help from my counselor and she cried the entire time. I hadn't realized how much of an impact a little hood girl could make on somebody's life as perfect as hers. I even had her husband and kids referring to Wal-Mart as 'Wally World', which was the funniest shit ever. After she told me that I could call her anytime that I needed to and to make sure that I kept in touch, we cried non-stop tears before I walked out and waited for Becka. When she pulled up, she wasn't dressed like the Becka I knew. She had a brand new car and she even had on a work uniform for Southwest Airlines. She looked... different, like more her age.

"Niecey Poohhhh!" She ran from her side of the car and embraced me. "You look so good Bari! I'm so proud of your for sticking with this program!" She pulled back and then hugged me again.

"Thanks aunt Becka." I smiled and wobbled my way to her car

while she grabbed my bags and tossed them in the trunk of her car. We pulled off and the questions begin... she wanted to know everything. *So how was it? What the sessions were like? Did they treat me good? Did I learn anything? Am I doing right and taking care of myself?* I answered every question without copping an attitude cause if the shoe were on the other foot I would've been just as curious. After I answered her, I had some questions of my own. "So you're working now?" I smiled.

She nod her head, "Yes girl... cause you know, after this whole situation with you it really had me thinkin' like I had to get my shit together and as soon as possible so I got me a new car, a new job, and I just been living the best I could. I'm in this program with these people to help me buy a house soon. Like your brother does the best he can but as women, either me or Sue should've been tryna be a better role model for you."

There was no denying what she was saying because it was certainly true, I didn't have that at all growing up. "I'm proud of you." I told her.

"We gonna be okay." She said still focusing on the road. When we pulled up to 'Da Nolia' I was overwhelmed with emotion, more than I had expected to be to the point that I didn't even wanna get out the car. I didn't have to say shit to aunt Becka cause she already knew what it was. "Listen, you don't owe nan muhfucka around here a goddamn thing okay? Not one explanation."

"I know.."

"Good, now I'ma drive you around back and we can go in through the back way but that's only for today Belcalis... we won't be doing this everyday."

I sighed. "Thank you..." that was such a relief cause I wasn't ready at all. Becka led me to my bedroom in her apartment that was set up all nice for me and I appreciated it. "Wait! You leaving?" I asked noticing her heading back out the door.

She nod her head, "Yep... I gotta work girl! It's dinner on the stove, you'll be fine just keep the doors locked. You ain't a baby Bari. I'll call you on my break." She rushed out.

Once again, I was all alone and while I may have been nervous; it did feel good as hell to be back home.

EIGHT

Hennessy (Nessy) Morales

I TOLD you over and over these niggas will fuck you and leave you so I don't know why you so mad now Nessy! It ain't like ya'll was together... okay so he has a baby and that's it. What did you think, you were always gonna be the only one? I don't understand what's the problem here! Bitch I'm more pissed that you dropped my fucking little cousin off over there and you have yet to go and get her!" My cousin Marie yelled in my ear as if I wasn't standing right in front of her. We were in the middle of my mama's living room about to have a show down!

AFTER I WENT to identify Monica that shit fucked me up pretty bad and I couldn't even go home. I even took some time off from work but Gu had me fucked up and his bitch did too! I wasn't expecting her to even be around this long but I guess I really pushed him away this time. I felt like I was losing it and it didn't make it no better that the bitch RaRa posted all of these pictures of Messiah Junior all over Facebook and Instagram. I was heated, the lil baby was handsome as fuck and he looked exactly like Messiah. One pic on Facebook got damn there a thousand likes and over 2k shares. Now the world knew that Messiah had a baby, and it just so happened to be a boy. "I WANTED A FUCKING SON MARIE!" I yelled.

"BITCH PLEASE! YOU SOUND CRAZY!" She snapped. We were both lucky that my mama nor Ramos was home because shit wouldn't have been going down like this, especially not in their house.

"HAVE A KID AND YOU'LL SEE!" I spat. "Oh my bad, a nigga never loved you enough!"

SMACK!

THE BITCH HIT me dead in my face now it was time to rumble. We must've tore the whole damn house up in this bitch! Blow for blow I took all my anger and frustrations out on her. I knew Marie could fight and she wasn't a pussy by a long shot cause we grew up fighting together. But this shit was long overdue anyway cause she was always in my fucking business, not to mention that I was grieving my fucking friend and I had to deal with her bullshit now. We must have fought until we were tired and couldn't swing no more. She got the best of me cause she sat her thick ass in my chest and refused to get up. "Get the fuck off of me!"

"BITCH YOU GO GET my lil cousin! And I fucking mean it or I'ma tell Ramos everything! Jodidamente loca, no enciendes a la familia!"

"OKAY! Okay! I'm going! Now get the fuck off of me!" I spat and struggled to get up.

"GOOD..." she adjusted her clothes and looked around. "Now first let's clean this shit up before they get here."

I DIDN'T SAY another word. We cleaned up the place in silence and I hopped in my car to make my way over to 'Da Nolia' to get my baby. I knew Messiah probably thought that I'd just left her on the doorstep but in reality, I was in the cut watching her. I didn't leave until I saw his bitch bring her inside to safety. I made my way up the flight of steps and banged on the door only to be greeted by some white boy. "Can I help you?" He asked.

I TRIED PEEKING around his shoulder. "I'm here to get my baby, where she at?" I frowned.

HE WORE a look of surprise on his face and looked me up and down like he was checking me out, only he looked disgusted. "Humph, well she's not here and shame on you to just dump your daughter off on a stoop because you're upset with the father for moving on and living his life."

WHO THE FUCK did he think he was? "I'm sorry? I didn't know my baby daddy hired a fucking door man but I'm pretty sure he pays you enough to mind your business."

HE CHUCKLED, "that's cute... really cute. However, I wont argue with a bitter baby mama. Your daughter isn't here. As a matter of fact she's out with Qui and Gu right now having some much needed family time as you requested. You know... Step mommy duties." He smiled.

THIS LIL FUCKER almost made me put my size seven in his slick ass mouth. "Yeah well I'll be back to get her! I didn't say she could live here, I only left her for a while so I could handle some business. Please don't greet me when I get back, I just might have to whoop your ass."

"HUNNY... it looks like your ass is already whipped. Goodbye." He slammed the door in my face. This little shit eater had me fucked up. I had a trick for him though, I was gone patiently wait outside until they arrived back home. In the meantime, I called Sue.

"SUE! Can you call your son for me since he's not answering my calls?" I asked.

"NOPE, I tell you over and over I don't get in the middle of that shit... but I heard you left my grandbaby on that doorstep, I outta whoop ya ass my damn self."

I SUCKED MY TEETH, "No I didn't, it ain't nothing like how they tryna make it seem and that's on GOD... I didn't leave till my baby was inside the apartment."

"WELL IT DON'T MATTER how it happened, point is... you losing yo damn mind all over a man who no longer wants you, and you so beautiful that you making yourself look ugly by doing all this tryna get his attention. You really think this gonna ever bring him back Nessy? Cause you wrong girl... it ain't gonna happen. You gotta move on!"

"I HAVE!" I lied.

"NO YOU DIDN'T... tell the lies to ya mami cause she gone believe you, not me."

"I CAN'T BELIEVE he had another baby!" I screamed.

"AND LET ME GUESS, you wanna go put him on child support now right?"

"I'M SERIOUSLY THINKING ABOUT IT!" I blurted.

"BUT WHY NESSY? He takes care of his child..."

"IT DOESN'T MATTER, I gotta go." I hung up on her. I watched that parking lot like a hawk waiting for them to pull up and when they did, I was on it. I didn't give a fuck that the whole hood was out. "Winter!" I smiled. "You ready to go?" I asked her walking up on them.

"NOOO MOMMY!" She cried. "Tomorrow we can go! I have to make cookies tonight." She pleaded with her lil eyes as she latched on to Gu's leg and held Qui's hand with the other. That sight broke my fucking heart, like what had I done. In a act of being malicious, I'd actually opened up the door for my daughter to take a liking to a woman I very much despised.

MESSIAH STOOD THERE with bags in his hand looking stone cold in the face. "Qui, take Winter upstairs."

THE MINUTE she started walking away with my child, I rushed them only to be stopped by Gu. "I'm warning you Nessy... get the fuck on." He said in a low tone. "Don't show out in front of my daughter cause she gone hate yo ass in the end, not me." He said ripping me with his words. In no time Qui and Winter were gone.

"JUST GIVE ME MY BABY." I begged.

"NAH, since you wanna play games, you can get her back when I say so. You got me fucked up kidd."

"GIVE ME MY DAMN BABY BACK!" I said a little louder this time. "HE'S A KIDNAPPER! SOMEBODY CALL 911!" I blurted out to the crowd and they all looked at me crazy.

"YOU MAKING yo'self look stupid as fuck right now yo." He said all calm like. This was some shit I wasn't used to, like why was he so calm? Why wasn't he acting out so I can get his ass locked up or something? Anything to get his ass back. If I couldn't have him, neither could his other baby mama. It pissed me off even more when I saw that the bags in his hands was baby shit, shit for a lil boy.

"ARHHHHHH!" I yelled and gripped my hair, "I hate you! I fucking hate you!"

HE SMIRKED, "yeah.. well fall in line with the rest of them hoes." He tried to walk off but I wasn't done. Boom! I kicked the passenger door of the Q50 they'd just gotten out of putting a dent in it.

"YEAH! What now nigga! Tell your bitch to come outside and catch this fade, ole weak ass hoe!" I yelled to the top floor hoping she could hear me. In all my distraction and frustrations, I hadn't even realized there was a cop on the block in a undercover car witnessing my rampage. I didn't know that shit cause this wasn't my hood. But that explained why Gu didn't act out like I thought he would. My rant didn't stop until I felt the cuffs being slapped on my wrist.

"YOU JUST PLAYED YA'SELF NESSY..." Gu shook his head, "told yo ass to chill."

THE OFFICER READING me my rights drowned his words out. Now not only did I embarrass myself, I was now about to be booked again and I was already out on bond. Wasn't this bout a bitch!

NINE

Rayliris (RaRa) Almanzar

WHOEVER SAID that raising a child was easy lied! While I was in love with my lil man, I was exhausted and tired and since Swain and Tricia were always gone during the day, I decided to stay at my aunt's place during the day so she could at least help me, especially after giving birth cause I swore my body was in shock after that. I felt like I was hit by a damn Mack truck; like I really took my hat off to women out there pushing these babies out like champs cause I couldn't do it. It was still hard to cope with the fact that I was just a 'baby mama' but I couldn't blame nobody but myself.

I RECEIVED a text from Gu telling me that he wanted to see him and dropped some stuff off and I told him it was okay and to just come to my aunt's house. Plus, I wanted to step out for a few to go run and pick some things up so he agreed to watch him for a lil bit. I was only four weeks postpartum and I knew I shouldn't have been out but being crammed in a apartment all day was killing me. I'd been hearing some rumors that his other baby mother had gotten locked up for some bullshit and even though she was out now, I didn't wanna stress him out. This shit needed to be smooth as possible for now. "Hey..." I spoke when I opened the door to let him in.

"WHERE MY BABY?" he asked walking past me not even speaking to me at all. He had two hands full of bags from 'Babies R Us' and 'The Children's Place' that he sat on the floor next to the couch.

"WELL ALRIGHTY THEN..." I closed the door and locked it back. "Bottles are in the fridge so all you have to do is heat them up when he's ready to eat and everything else he needs is in the back room. Don't forget to burp him after he eats..."

HE CUT me off and spoke without even looking at me, instead he picked his son up from the bassinet. "RaRa, this ain't my first child. I know what to do... I don't need a whole lesson, I practically raised Winter... Nessy didn't have to do shit."

FUNNY that he would say something like that, especially when I was waking up in the middle of the night on my own with no help from him. "Well my bad... this isn't yo first time but it is mine."

"YEAH, WHATEVER..." He sat down and flicked the TV on to the game.

"WHAT TIME WILL YO auntie be here?"

"SHE'S NORMALLY HERE HELPING me but she had an hair appointment so probably not until later. I wont be long though."

HE NOD his head and it bothered the shit outta me that he wouldn't even look at me. All I wanted was to be loved, shit, by some fucking body and I rather it had been from him but for some reason, he just wouldn't open up to me. I closed the door and locked it making my way to my car. The fist stop was to the hair store to get some weave to get my hair braided because I was tired of wearing this damn silk Louie scarf on my head. After that I made my way to sprint to pay my phone bill and the final stop was to the market to buy something to cook. I hoped Gu stayed for dinner to watch the baby for me so I could do that.

PUSHING the cart down the aisle, I loaded my cart up since my stamps had just hit so I didn't have to hesitate about what could come and what couldn't come. I was halfway down the meat line when a little pretty girl with gorgeous hair ran past me. "Qui over here!" She stopped in front of one of the freezers where they had hot pockets and pizzas.

"WINTER!" the pretty girl yelled hitting the corner. "I told you not to run off." She giggled just as she made eye contact with me. From the look in her face, I knew that she knew exactly who I was. She cleared her throat and kept walking. "Which ones?" She asked Gu's daughter.

SHE POINTED at the ham and cheese pockets. "I want theseeee!" She sang.

IN THE PIT of my stomach, I was sick as fuck... Gu never let me around his daughter, ever! And this chick Qui had such a free spirit about her that it was hard not to like her but I couldn't help the jealousy of watching an entire scenario that I really wished was me. I was the one with his son and he had yet introduce her to her little brother. Hell, I wasn't even sure if she knew that she even had a little brother. I bit my lip until I felt the blood draw in order to stop from saying anything out of the way or be malicious but it was really hard.

I KNEW she sensed that I wanted to say something cause I was horrible with tryna hide the look on my face. Yet and still, I pushed on with a hurt heart and bitter ass feelings. "Aye... hold up!" I heard the girl Qui yell from behind me. I spun around and waited; I felt the sweat on my hands as I tightly gripped the handle of that cart.

"YEAH..." I asked dryly.

"I KNOW YOU ARE." She said looking over her shoulder to make sure that Winter was still in eye sight not paying her any mind.

"OKAY...AND?"

"CONGRATULATIONS ON YOUR SON... he's very handsome."

"OKAY... THANKS." I shrugged.

AND THEN HER entire demeanor changed. "You showed up to my job when you were pregnant. You were real rude to me for no reason, but I get it. Gu is a good dude so why wouldn't you be bitter? I just want yo to know that any more games you're cooking up in that head to play... forget it cause I'm not going no where and neither is he."

"ARE we talking about the same man who's at my house right now watching our son?" I asked sarcastically.

SHE NOD HER HEAD, "Yep sounds about right, I'm actually here getting dinner right now because he called and requested his favorite meal... me with a little strawberries on top... of course I ran out of strawberries from his last request so I'm here getting more. See..." She smiled and pointed at her basket.

THIS FUCKING BITCH! I wanted to yell and scream and just kick the fucking aisle over! This stupid, cocky, arrogant fucking bitch! "Yeah whatever." I said instead. "He ain't gone do shit but fuck you and leave you like he do everyone else... now if you don't mind, I have a precious baby that I share with 'YOUR' man to get back to."

"THAT'S FINE." She smiled. "Take care."

SHE WALKED AWAY with so much confidence it made me even madder. Watching her grip Winter's hand again had me in my feelings to. She should've been getting to know me and her lil brother... not some fucking girlfriend who probably wouldn't be around in a year any fucking way. By the time I left the store, I was in tears. I wanted to scream! I wanted to smoke a fat ass joint! I wanted to fuck! Be held or something! I needed some dick in my life like now and right now! Anything to relieve this stress! I had been so faithful to Gu in our imaginary ass relationship while I was carrying his child that I didn't even have not one fucking man whose dick I could jump on... NOT FUCKING ONE!

THERE WAS one place I did know that I could go and the timing was perfect! "Swain!" I stripped from all my clothes at the front door of his apartment since I knew Tricia wouldn't have been home until later on! "Swain! Where you at?!" I walked through the hall but ass naked with tears in my eyes. I found him in the room laying there with his boxers on exposing the huge print of his dick with his fine ass. I knew I was dead ass wrong for what I was about to do, but if I didn't do this... I was gonna lose it! I needed the touch from man and Gu wouldn't touch me.

SWAIN SAT up drooling through his eyes but at the same time, he looked at me like I was crazy. "What's wrong wit'chu mayne?"

INSTEAD OF ANSWERING... I rushed to him like a animal in heat and plastered kisses all over him while straddling his dick professionally using my feet to get his boxers down and over his rock hard dick. "Just fuck me Swain." I begged with tears in my eyes grinding on his bare dick.

HE TRIED to make some sense of this situation but his dick did more talking for him. "What's wrong RaRa?" He asked in between kisses. "That nigga did somethin' to you mayne?"

"NO!" I snapped taking control. "Shhh." I licked on his neck and used one hand to place his dick inside of my silky opening. "Ouuuu-uu!" I squealed as he filled me up no longer fighting.

HE GRIPPED my hips while I rode him buck wild looking at the pleasure on his face. "Goddammmm!" he groaned with his eyes shut fucking me as hard as I was fucking him. My breast bounced up and down and the sweat trickled from both of our bodies. It had been a long ass time since I sex and I was allowing the anger and frustrations vent through my pussy and right now he was a lucky nigga cause this was the first and last time he'd ever get this pussy so I was glad he was enjoying. "Shit Ra! Nigga bout to Nut!!!"

I TUNED out the smacking sounds and focused on my pussy feeling the explosion coming my damn self. "Ahhhhhhh! Shittttt!" I closed my eyes and vibrated all over that dick as our juices exploded together. I was out of energy but I felt relieved as my head feel on his chest tryna catch my breath. "Thank you." I whispered.

THE FRONT DOOR slammed causing us both to jump. "Oh shit, was that here or upstairs?" He asked.

"I'M NOT SURE." I aid hopping up rushing for my clothes.

SWAIN WENT to check the door. "It's unlocked... you locked it when you came in?" he asked confused.

"YEAH! AT LEAST I THINK SO." I put my clothes back on and grabbed my keys.

SWAIN LOOKED AT ME CRAZY. "You wanna tell me what the fuck goin' on RaRa?"

I PUSHED PAST HIM, I hadn't even washed myself up and I knew my hair was threw. I knew I looked like a disaster. "No.... I gotta go get my son... lock up." I rushed out leaving him stuck. when I finally made it to the parking lot I was greeted by the sounds of rubber burning and screeching out of the parking lot. I was thinking that maybe it was one of the lil young boys but when I looked up, all I caught were the tail lights of Tricia's car. My heart dropped!

I NOW KNEW that the sounds of the door slamming was from her and I never meant to hurt my friend. I hopped in my car and called her over and over but she didn't pick up one time, which was scary cause Tricia was one of those people who got you when you least expected it. I knew she was hurt right now and because of that, she wouldn't confront me while I was expecting it. I immediately called Swain as I sped to my aunt's house. "Swain! Tricia knows..." I cried.

"YEAH, I know and because of you I just lost my girl... stay away from me ole sneaky ass bitch! Or I promise I'ma kill you!" I snapped. "You better hope I get her back! I didn't initiate that shit, you came over here and practically shoved a niggas dick inside of you..." he sighed. "Man bye RaRa... get you some fucking help yo."

I DIDN'T EVEN bother to call him back cause I was dead ass wrong. I tried my best to get myself together before I walked in my aunt's house but it must've been an epic failure. Gu was on the couch still holding MJ but he had bathed and changed his clothes into some PJ's. "Thanks Gu." I rushed my baby boy, you can go now."

HE LOOKED at me sideways and examined me real good. "You look like shit... and you smell like dick..." he frowned. "Mayne you's fuckin' hoe RaRa forreal. Go wash yo ass before you touch my boy."

I SUCKED my teeth and stormed off, "whatever I do with my pussy is MY Business Gu! Shit, you don't want it so whatever!" I slammed the bathroom door and took a quick shower. When I was finished and dressed, he was more than willing to hand me my baby.

"DON'T KISS HIM EITHER." He turned his nose up and walked out. I locked the door behind him and stared down in my son's face. What the fuck was I doing? Why was I so distraught over a nigga that didn't want me, and so distraught that I was willing to fuck up other people's happiness cause I couldn't come to terms with finding my own. My son deserved a good life and a good mother and I needed to get my shit together. I washed how he squirmed in my arms and yawned allowing me to smell his baby breath.

"I'M GONNA DO BETTER SON..." I promise. I kissed his cheek glad that Gu wasn't here to see it. This shit was all fucked up.

TEN

Turquoise Qui Edwards

'Girl I wanna see you twerk, I'll throw a lil money if you twerk, ion really think you can twerk, if you broke go to work, make that big booty twerk, can I touch that booty? That big ole booty, shake that booty, can I lay on the floor, Mike Tyson that booty, copyright that booty, I just wanna see you twerk'

"OMG! Edwards what exactly is this song?" Hulk turned his nose up while giggling at the same time. For the first time in a long time, I had finally gotten away from the stress of my everyday life and just enjoyed some good ass college partying. The Omega Center was super thick and everybody from the local colleges came out to support DJ Rhymer on his new Mix-tape release party. I playfully put a arch in my back and started twerking my ass off to 'Blac Youn-sta's' latest hit.

"Look Hulk! It's like this!" I bounced my booty up and down in front of him.

"Just look at that thing." He sneered. "How in the world do you do that? It's like a big bowl of Jello and has a mind of it's own." He giggled using one of his finger poking at it.

"You don't know what you're missing Hulk! Women are beautiful!" I yelled over the music.

He waved me off, "Hunny, a woman has nothing that I want okay? I said it once and I'll say it again. I don't swim in the fish market."

"Whatever!" I laughed checking the time. "Shit! I was supposed to meet Gu an hour ago and you've got me all in here twerking."

"No ma'am... your ass has you in here twerking. Literally." He grabbed me by the hand and led the way out of the building. We were driving his car tonight. "I'm not crashing at your place tonight Edwards."

"But whyyyy?" I sang. I had gotten used to him crashing on my sofa every other night or whenever he and Jonathan got angry with each other. I lived for those nights cause to hear them arguing and going back and forth was the funniest shit I'd ever seen in my life. Hell, Hulk had been around 'Da No' so long that by this point, that everyone around there knew him on a first name basis now.

"Because just like you, I have a man too, and we made up." He flashed a quick smile as we fought our way through the outside crowd. I saw plenty of faces from the hood, including Bambi but she was too far from me for me to speak, and she was hustling making her money so I didn't bother her.

"Whatever... ughhh." I frowned plopping my ass in the passenger seat of his car.

Hulk ignored me and headed back to the apartment. It was still early and the hood was lit per usual but I didn't care about none of them, my main concern was Gu. Of course I found him on the block rolling dice as usual, which I was glad to see cause after he visited with Beans earlier, I knew he was real down about it and he wanted his homey home with him. I promised I was gonna be by his side and do whatever he needed me to do and when he'd give me money to send to Beans, I made sure that I sent it to Rain as well although she never acknowledged me and wrote me to say thank you or nothing; not that I did it for that cause I didn't... I did it cause no matter how much of a fucked up person she was, she was still my sister.

"So you're really not coming in?" I frowned.

Hulk shook his head, "nope... going home for some much needed make up sex."

"OMG too much damn information." I laughed and then reached over kissing him on the cheek. "Well call me later on or tomorrow. It's a must that we study cause next week is gonna be crazy."

After he pulled off, I sat on the stoop and just watched my man instead of going in the apartment since I didn't wanna be in there alone and Winter was with Sue. I really didn't understand where her and Gu's relationship stood right now, all I knew was it was weird as hell... like they talked, but they didn't talk. Sitting there actually made me think about Se myself cause while I may have been with Gu, I never had no one on one time with her. I think my legs had a mind of their own when I found my way in front of Sue's door knocking on it. "Who is it?!" the door swung open and I was face to face with my hopefully, one day, mother-in-law.

I let off a nervous smiles thinking about how dumb I must have looked, I was at this lady's door and didn't even know why or what I wanted to say. "Hey Ms. Carter." I smiled.

Her eyes lit up, like she was just glad to have some company. She was just too fucking pretty to me... even with all her flaws. "What my son do? That's the only time one of his girls come knock on this door and I don't get in the middle of his shit; I'll keep saying it until everybody understand where I'm comin' from."

I nod my head, "I understand... he hadn't done nothing to me." I smiled.

She stepped to the side, "Well happy wife, happy life and if that's the case then come on in." She stepped to the side and allowed me in her apartment with no other questions. I quickly scanned the place enjoying her cute lil setup that she had going on. It smelled good too and that was a plus. "Don't be too loud cause my grandbaby is back there sleep and I don't want her waking up." She shook her head and chuckled. "That damn girl is busy as hell... ohhh child and could talk yo ear off."

"Yeah..." I laughed. "I already know, but she's so fun to have around. I'ma be sad when she leaves to go back to her mama."

"Take a seat..." Sue pointed to her table and then her couch. "It's plenty of room to sit down in here, you ain't gotta stand up by no door." I didn't wanna go sit at the table cause that was too far from her and I didn't want her to think I was acting saddity so I sat on the couch where I'd be closer to her instead. For the next few minutes she just gave me this awkward ass look examining me. "You know, you real pretty, you're a very beautiful girl."

"Thank you." I smiled.

"So how did you do it?" She asked catching me off guard.

"Do what?"

"You know, get Gu to wanna settle down? Last person that I saw him try to settle down with was Nessy, but that crazy girl drove the poor boy crazy. Now all the other little flings... he didn't care about none of them girls and that's why I told them don't come to my door crying. Hell, you don't like the way he moving with you then stop giving the pussy up... simple."

I fell out laughing, "You just too cool."

"Hell, I'm real hunny... I ain't old I'm hip to the game, but when it come to you though... it's different even the way he look at you. A man don't gotta tell you or nobody else how he feel about you but the way he looks, or talks about that woman will tell it all... just gotta read in between the lines."

I nod my head. "I feel the same exact way about him too... trust me."

"Well you still ain't answered my question." She carried on.

I shrugged and got a little more relaxed talking to her, "to be honest, Gu and me got together by default. He wasn't even suppose to like me."

"What, was he supposed to kill you?" She asked.

I furrowed my brows, "Huh?"

This time she shrugged, "I mean hey, this is my son that we're talking about and I know my son so if your first encounter with him came from a bad place... spare me the details. I ain't never tryna be no accessory to shit."

This lady literally had me cracking the fuck up, I should've come to sit with her long ago. "Okay, I'll spare you the details then... but just know where we are now, it's all love."

She squint her eyes, "for how long though?"

I didn't quite understand her question but I replied anyway. "For as long as we'd like... if that's what you're asking me cause I'm not sure."

She sighed. "Look, I know that my son and me aren't in the best place right now, which is fine cause every family has their problems but I love my boy. And on top of that, he's a real good person. Now, I know that you clearly know he has two kids and two crazy ass baby mama's and it's gon' take a strong woman to stand in that paint."

"I'm aware." I spoke up.

"Nah... are you?" She quizzed not waiting for an answer. "Cause it's gonna take a strong woman to stick by his side and understand that he's the type of man that will love you with no limits and do whatever to keep you happy; he wont disrespect you or let nobody else disrespect you for that matter so if you don't think you can handle his life, then don't be with him... just leave him now cause if you hurt my son, I'm coming for you." She chuckled but there was a message behind that and the way she beat the shit outta Bari... I was sure she'd try that shit with me, especially about Gu.

"Trust me, I have no plans on leaving that man unless that's something we both agreed to for our own reasons, and trust me when I tell you that I'm not letting nobody run me off. To be honest with you, it only makes us closer... every time one of the kids mama's start some foolishness."

"Say shit..." she frowned.

"What?"

"You said foolishness when in reality you wanted to say shit. Am I right?"

"Absolutely."

She laughed again, "okay then, say what's on your mind, you never have to sugar coat shit around me, just be you at all times cause it's not enough people doing that now days."

"I got you... so yeah, like I was saying; it makes us closer every time one of the kids mama's started some shit."

"That's what I'm talking about!" She high fived me and sat back down.

"Have you met his son yet?" I asked.

She shook her head, "nope and I don't plan to see him until his daddy starts bringing him around on his own. I don't feel like I should have to communicate with these women that I barely even know all because they're trying to have some kind of connection with me in order to keep him."

I cleared me throat. "Oh, is that what you think of me?"

"Not at all." She said standing up to go to her bar and pour her a shot of Hennessy. "Have some?" She asked.

"No ma'am... I'm fine."

"Yeah... it's best that way." she downed a shot and then. "This stuff is poison."

"So thy do you drink it?" I questioned.

"Because I have too... this is how I cope. I have a daughter that hates me and a son who needs me no matter how hard he tries to be."

I didn't wanna too much touch on that cause it was too early on for me to be discussing her kids with her and I didn't wanna say the wrong shit that would have her pissed with me.

"They love you..." I told her. "Sometimes we don't know how to accept the different ways our parents come at us about something but it don't mean that because we may not agree that we don't love ya'll. We only get one mama.

She nod her head and agreed. "I like you even more now that I've spoken to you."

"Well thanks Ms. Carter... I like you too."

"Un un girl call me Sue. I'm not with the Ms. Carter stuff, makes me feel so old."

"I go you... I'ma keep that in mind." I stood up and placed my arms above my head to stretch.

"You hungry?" She asked. "Whenever Winter is here I always gotta make sure I cook hot meals."

Come to think of it, I was kinda hungry too; I was just ignoring the rumbling in my stomach and was just gonna find something at home and eat. "Um yeah, I'll take a plate."

Sue nod her head. "It's not much, some backed chicken, mash potatoes, and string beans."

My mouth watered, sounded good to me. "Oh yes... please. I am kind of starving."

Sue fixed my plate and even say down and ate with me while we talked a little more. There was one subject that I noticed she completely stayed away from and that was Bari. I wanted to ask her so badly if she would ever forgive her or even try to fix that relationship or get to try to know her grandson when she had the baby, but again, I didn't wanna overstep my boundaries. At the same time, although I didn't have no beef with my parents; shit was still sensitive in our lives so I couldn't play doctor to nobody else and their situation; I just couldn't.

When we were done eating, she packed me a plate to go for Gu and walked me out to the stoop. "Thanks again.... It was nice talking to you." I told her.

"Any time... don't be no stranger." She said before walking back inside of her apartment where Winter was still sleeping at.

I watched her backside until she disappeared and then I turned to walk away running into Bambi. I always wondered what the hell was in the snacks she sold to the entire hood but tonight, I wanted to try one. "Bambi!" I got her attention.

"Hey girl." She spoke while counting her money that she'd just collected from somebody.

"Hey... how much are the treats?" I asked.

Her head shot up. "You want a treat?"

"Is that surprising?" I chuckled.

She laughed too, always in a good spirit. "Well look... I have all kind of treats and they're called 'faded snacks' by the way." She paused to pull some out and show me. "Now the shit is good and all, all of them but you gotta eat them slow, especially if you ain't no smoker you gotta nibble on them cause the weed in this shit goes directly to your bloodstream." She warned.

"Damnnn it's like that?" I teased.

She nod her head, "yep, ask bout me... I don't play."

"Okay." I looked down in her box. "Let me get a treat, a brownie, a cookie, annnnnddddd." I continued to search looking for one more I didn't mind trying. "A cupcake."

She packed everything up for me and placed it inside of a small bag and gave it to me. "That's $35."

I reached down in my pocket and gave her 50 instead. "Thanks Bam." I waved her off and made it inside of the apartment where Gu was now sitting on my couch bare chest and looking good enough to eat as the lamp light bounced from his face to his stomach and chest.

He smiled when he saw me, "where you snuck off to?"

"I was talking to your mama... and she sent you a plate." I said unwrapping the foul so I could heat it up for him.

His demeanor didn't change at all, "Is that right?" he stroked his goatee.

I nod my head, "yep... she was cool though... and I got us some treats from Bambi."

He chuckled, "awe mayne... yo ass bout to be high as a kite!"

He joked and picked up his ringing phone. Since I didn't know who it was, I just listened. "What you thought it was a game when I said I was filing for legal visitation for both of mine? Yeah well you should've thought about that shit Nessy. Of course I'ma give her back, when I feel like it... right now, I'm enjoyin' my daughter."

When I gave him his plate I tried hard to listen to hear what

Nessy was saying since I figured out that's who it was calling but it was no use so I walked off. When I turned around, Gu was watching me intensely while he gripped his dick and bit down on his bottom lip like he was ready to give it to me right there on the spot.

"Nah... I filed one on RaRa too, fuck you mean mayne. I'm not playin' no more games with none of ya'... period. Yeah, well I guess I'll see you in court." He hung up and I didn't ask him any questions. One of my rules were to never bring up his baby mother's names under either one of our roofs unless we absolutely had too cause there was no way I was giving them that much power, or even mentioning them giving him a reason to even think about them, neither one.

After he finished eating his food, I washed dishes and cleaned the kitchen.

"When you done... meet me in the room in ya birthday suit lil mama." He licked his lips. Nigga need that in his life." Gu told me leaving me standing there with a wet pussy and jumping walls. I couldn't wait to get some of that good-good tonight. On God, I swear his shit was like crack and even the thought of him sharing it with someone else made me gag. I turned out all the lights and rushed in the room, only to find his ass knocked out on top of the covers.

I smile spread across my face and loved filled my heart just looking at him. He'd get a pass for pulling this stunt tonight cause I knew for a fact that he was tires and hadn't really caught up on no good sleep. I made my way over to him and draped the covers over his body and then kissed him before I decided to sit in the living room and nibble on one of my faded snacks while watching TV. I knew she said eat it slow, but the shit was so flavor able that before I knew it, the whole cookie was gone and I was literally floating to another dimension. My eyes were blood shot red and shit was spinning in front of me. I couldn't believe that I'd gotten that damn high. The only choice I had was to ball up on the couch and sleep.

In the middle of the night, I found myself over the toilet throwing up a lung... tryna be fucking fast; never again! The shit was good and all but I was done experimenting. Gu could have all the damn snacks he wanted cause I had officially retired and that shit wasn't for me. After cleaning myself up... I stood up and got myself together so I could go and snuggle up next to Gu's warm body... some shit his baby mama's were mad they couldn't do. If they were smart they'd be nice to me cause I wasn't bad at all and even when their were times that they couldn't contact Gu and needed something; I was the one that could make it happen. "I love you Gu." I whispered in his ear.

He rolled over and placed me on his chest. "I love you too lil mama." He said in his sleepy voice. "Shhhh... go to sleep."

ELEVEN

Messiah Gu Carter

'Dear son'

"GRANNA, I know you wanna sit and hold the boy all day but we gotta go. I still got a few more stops before I give him back to his mama... I promise I'mma bring him back next week." I laughed tryna convince granna to give me MJ. From the moment we walked through her door and she saw his little face up close and in person, she was in love. She had fifty million questions about how in the hell did he make it into this world before I arrived but since I'd been here, she didn't ask not one of those question.

"HE SHO IS a cute and handsome little baby; don't matter if his mama is some kind of hoe... together ya'll made a beautiful baby..."

She snuggled her nose into his neck causing him to squirm. I knew if he could talk he'd tell granna to fall back and leave him alone. Poor kid been getting swarmed with so much love, he didn't even have time to rest. "Where is him and his mama living at right now Messiah? Wherever it is, I know you making sure he's safe aren't you?"

I GRABBED a peppermint from her candy bowl and popped it in my mouth. "Yeah, she was stayin' in a better neighborhood with her best friend but they had some kind of fall out for whatever reason so now she's been back stayin' at her aunt house fulltime. I play my part though." I assured her.

"NOW MESSIAH, what you do for one child, you have to do for the other." Granna furrowed her brows looking at me displeased.

"SHEITTTT...EXCUSE my language granna but fuck that... I refuse to take care of RaRa... especially after how she did me."

"OH BOY... please... you gonna have to let that go one day in order to have a healthy co-parenting relationship."

I WASN'T HEARING that shit, as much as I loved granna... I just wasn't doing it. "We good how we are right now and matter fact; I'm the only one actually taking care of MJ since his mama don't have a job."

"WELL WHAT DOES she do with herself then?" Granna asked now helping me to repack his bag.

I SHRUGGED, "Ion know, she go to school or somethin' like that."

I HONESTLY THOUGHT RaRa was gone trip when I asked her to pick lil man up but much to my surprise, she was all for it. Guess she was tryna stay clean faced with me since she needed my money and she didn't wanna end up in the same boat with Hennessy. I agreed to keep him for the day since Qui had work and school and plus I got tired of having to sit up under RaRa's triflin' ass every time I wanted to see my son, that was the most aggravating shit ever. I was mad that my time was over with him, but I was sending him back with a bunch of shit and a lot of love. The only thing I was still hesitant about was telling Winter cause I always promised her since she was born that it was just gon' always be me and her and I didn't want my baby to feel betrayed like daddy lied to her or some shit. Then there was the part of me that thought, maybe she would be happy. Kids loved other kids especially when they were the oldest but fuck it; I wasn't gone stress about it... only time would tell.

GRANNA GAVE MJ at least five more cheek kisses after I had him strapped in the car in order to keep away to keep him from getting five more, I had to go. "Aiight granna! I'll call you later on!" I yelled out the window and drove off. I bopped my head to the music but I didn't turn it up cause I didn't wanna fuck with MJ's little ears, that didn't stop him from squirming though. But that was pretty much all he did cause in reality, he was a good baby and the only times he cried was when he was wet, shitted, or hungry. From what RaRa said, he even slept through the night but I wasn't ready for the over night thing yet though; that shit came with time.

"YO?" I answered my phone for an unknown caller.

SILENCE.

"YO?" I said again.

"AM I ON SPEAKERPHONE?" The female asked. I didn't recognize her voice at all.

"MAYNE, WHO THE FUCK IS THIS?" I asked again getting real agitated.

"IT DOESN'T EVEN MATTER. I know ya baby mama a bird and all, but I'm gonna need you to either be a family with her, or start back fucking her so she can stay away from my fucking man! Ole trifling ass bitch!"

CLICK.

"WHAT THE FUCK?" I frowned and tossed the phone in the passenger seat, I didn't even know which one of these baby mama's she was talking about but if I had to put my money on it; I'd say she's probably talkin' about RaRa cause Hennessy was crazy but she ain't never been on no hoe shit. I don't even know why I got a phone call about it cause RaRa wasn't my girl. I made one last stop before I headed over to Bravo to meet up with RaRa since that was our meet up spot for pick up today while she ran errands.

WHEN I PULLED UP, she still wasn't here yet, so I took my son out of his seat and held him until she got there. I know he was real little and he didn't understand, but I felt strongly in my heart about the bond that I was building with him. He just didn't know it yet. My mind drifted to Sue for a second cause I knew that granna was gone tell her that she met MJ, and then Sue was gone be feelin' some type of way. Truth was, I just wanted Sue and me to be on a better communication level before I brought him around. Winter was different cause she was already established and she knew her family very well. MJ, however, was a little different and I to wait before I formally introduced him to everybody else... even Qui. She wasn't trippin' though, and she didn't nag me about it cause she knew I wasn't tryna hide nothin' from her. See, Qui understood me and I understood her... we both complimented each other and that's what made her so different from the rest of those bitches.

I PEEPED RaRa speeding in the parking lot but I didn't know what the fuck for, she was already late anyway. She hopped out looking like her old self again. Her hair was freshly done and she was rocking a one piece bodysuit that showed all her curves. I was still a nigga so I had to admit that the baby weight did her body a lot of good... but still, I didn't want that shit or the problems that came with it. "Sorry I'm late." She said walking up to my car smelling like some kind of fruity spray that tickled my nose.

"SAY RA... WHO NIGGA YOU FUCKIN'?" I quizzed.

"WHAT?" She frowned. "I'm not fucking nobody nigga... I'm not fucking period." She licked her lips. "I been waiting for you."

I SHOOK MY HEAD, "You'll never taste this dick again mayne... get that shit out ya head. Now who nigga you fuckin'?" I asked again.

SHE ROLLED her eyes upwards and sighed, "I'm not fucking nobody man Gu."

"SHIT, that ain't what I heard, but shit you say you ain't so that's what I'ma stick to."

"WHY YOU CARE?" She shrugged.

"YOU KNOW BETTER... and you know I give no fucks... when ya ass cut off, you cut the fuck off... simple."

"WHATEVER." She mumbled no longer able to disguise her attitude, not that I gave a damn. "How was your day?"

I GRABBED MJ from his seat and went to strap him in the seat inside of RaRa's car instead. Then I went and popped the trunk and grabbed all the bags I had for him along with his diaper bag. "Any time I spend with my son is always beautiful." I told her and then leaned down in her car to adjust MJ's lil cap on his head... the weather was bout to drop tonight and I didn't want him catching no cold. "The weather bout to drop, I hope you takin' him home."

"I MIGHT HAVE A FEW MORE ERRANDS." She said testing me.

I GAVE her one more look to let her know I wasn't playin' with her ass. "Take him the fuck home... or he can stay wit' me."

"OH MY GOD GU! I'm going home okay? Damn! Just cause I got a baby from you don't mean you run my life!"

"YO, YOU HEARD WHAT I SAID." I remained solid on my word, wasn't no take backs or switching up and I didn't give a fuck what she thought.

"SPEAKING of hearing what you said... I heard you loud and clear when I got the paper in the mail about you filing for visitation... you didn't have to do that shit... I told you that."

"OH YES THE fuck I did.. soon as ya'll get mad at a nigga the first thing ya'll wanna do is run to child support or try to take a baby away that a nigga don't mind spending time with or takin' care of. I don't have time for that shit so I'm changin' the game... I'm not playin' with none of ya. And when I get a wife, if we have a kid her ass goin' on papers too. I don't give a fuck if we all in the same house hold. I no longer trust women when it comes to these kids." I looked her up and down and chuckled. "Damn sho don't trust yo ass."

"YOU'RE FUCKING SICK." She hissed and chuckled at the same time.

I LOOKED AT HER SIDEWAYS, "says the person who poked multiple holes in a condom to get pregnant?"

SILENCE.

"YEAH, I THOUGHT SO." I said walking off. "Let me know when ya'll make it home so I can know my son is safe."

"OKAY, I'LL TEXT YOU."

I SAT in my car trying to wait for her to pull off but she was taking too long. Look like MJ probably started cuttin' up so she had to get him situated real quick. Being that I needed to hit the corner store and then go make a money move before I met Qui at the house, I had to go so I blew the horn and pulled off and now that MJ was out the car, I could enjoy my music too. Future and Chris Brown played all throughout the car.

'I TURN a side piece to a 9 piece, she out lying it shouldn't even matter she mine, I told her baby fuck it up one time, baby fuck it up one time, It's your birthday go ahead and out that cake on me, diamonds and zeros, I'll be your hero, ain't no cape on me, all you niggas lame, I ain't gotta pay shit, you know talk is cheap, aint talkin' money ain't no conversating, I've been leanin' all day, I'm faded, and she been fiendin' all day but can't take dick, I said baby fuck it up one time'

FOR WHATEVER ODD REASON, the store was on smash today, like some first of the month type shit and niggas was tryna get that Gwap. Meanwhile, all I needed to do was run in this bitch to get a Back Wood and bounce but niggas was makin' it real hard with Gu this and Gu that. "Yo Gu!" Pete called my name as soon as I left out the store, my lil dude was post up on his truck twirling a black and mild between his fingers, nigga was fresh as usual. Made me feel like a proud big brother or some shit. I walked up to him and gave him a pound hating that I left my hoodie in the car, shit, it was getting' cold as fuck already. "Cashhh monayyyy." I gave him a brotherly hug. "The fuck you doin' in town college boy?"

HE GRILLED me with his Golds, "Nah, you the one wit' all the money mayne." He chuckled. "But nah, I had to come in town for a few days to make a money move..." then he paused.

"NIGGA WHAT? SAY IT." I chuckled lookin' at him side ways.

"NAH, it's just you know Bari bout to have the baby any day now and I promised her that I was gon' be around for it. She was scared to be alone and shit."

I NOD MY HEAD, "Is that right?"

"YEAH." He shrugged.

"SO WHAT YA'LL TRYNA DO?" I asked him.

"SHIT... NOTHIN' mayne. I told her I'ma always be there and I keep my word."

"AND HOW YA girl feel about it?"

"SHIT, she in her bag but she'll be aiight."

I NOD MY HEAD AGAIN. "I feel you..." I couldn't lie and say I didn't miss Bari and I honestly could forgive her for all that shit with Tuff. The hardest thing for me to accept was that Ronnie shit but even lookin' at Pete still bein' by her side, he was actually helpin' me to register the thought of forgiveness and one day it was gon have to come but that time was gon' have to come when I was ready for it and who the fuck knew when that was gone be? "Aiight mayne... get at me before you leave." I gave him another pound to the fist and he did the same. As I prepared to walk off though, the screeching of tires hitting the corner had everybody's attention wondering in somebody was takin' the police on a chase cause it damn sho sounded like it.

MUCH TO MY SURPRISE, it was RaRa's car going full speed on the dash flying past the store with a black beat up Oldsmobile right on her ass. "THE FUCK!" I took off, the only thing I could think about was my son! Pete didn't ask no questions, he hopped in the Hummer and followed behind me as I almost broke the dash watching in horror as both cars swerved in and out of traffic at a very high rate. Pete was right behind me, my lil nigga wasn't lettin' up at all. My intentional thoughts was somebody was tryna rob her but what the fuck did she have? She ain't have shit.

EVEN THROUGH THE swerving and honking and reckless driving. I managed to call RaRa's phone. "COME ON RA! ANSWER THE FUCKING PHONE!" I bounced in the seat making sure my gun was in my lap. All I needed her to do was pull over and I could deal with whoever was behind the wheel of that car, but I couldn't shoot now the way they swerved in and out of traffic and risk sending a bullet in her car, not with my son in there! "FUCK!" I yelled missing a pedestrian by an inch, thank God she hopped out the way in the nick of time. "COME ON RA! I KNOW YOU SCARED MAN! JUST PULL OVER AND I GOT YOU!" I said out loud and hit the steering wheel. I was gonna have to get up on the side of the car and try to ram that bitch off the road but the way these cars were set up, it wasn't happening. They hit another corner and this time RaRa's car was on two wheels. "Shit!" Beads of sweat trickled down my forehead and I was running out of time and she was gone wreck the fuck out tryna get away from the fuckin' maniac. I felt shit in the pit of my stomach, I felt like I wanted to fucking vomit watching this shit play out.

PETE CALLED and I answered on the dash. "Pete!"

"YO WHAT THE FUCK GOIN' on mayne!" He swerved still right behind me but even I could here the panic in his voice and he didn't even know what was going on, neither did I.

"LOOK like my baby mama in some trouble mayne! And my fuckin' baby in the car!"

"WHAT!" He barked. "Mayne it's too many cars and they swervin' too much! We gotta barricade that muhfucka and block em off!"

"LET'S GO!" I disconnected the call with Pete now on the side of me. We both took outside lanes in hoped that we could barricade the car in the middle. Just when I thought I had a good shot to shoot a fuckin' tire out... that muhfucka swerved again and almost lost control. I saw the disaster before it even happened. "NOOOOOO!" I cried watching the horrific sight in front of me as the car clipped RaRa causing her car to go head on with the pole and burst into flames! Metal flew everywhere, the Oldsmobile hit a fire hydrant and so hard the tires flew off, a couple of cars came to a screeching stop trying not to be involved in the pile up and the rest of the cars... it was no use, they couldn't stop in time. I looked on in shock looking at the scene of fire, blood, guts, and shredded metal.

PETE RUSHED to the car and opened the driver door. "Gu!" I heard him but I couldn't respond. "Gu!" I was dazing out.

ALL I COULD SEE WERE the last images of memory that I had with MJ before I past the fuck out.

TO BE CONTINUED....

Would you like to stay in touch?

Facebook: Shalaine Yvonne Powell
Facebook: Authoress S. Yvonne
Facebook Reader's Group: Book Tea's The Readers Club
Instagram: Authoress_S.Yvonne

Email: Shalaine_Presents@yahoo.com

Please feel free to also join my mailing list by texting
ShalainePresents to 22828

SUBSCRIBE

Text Shan to 22828 to stay up to date with new releases, sneak peeks, contest, and more....

WANT TO BE A PART OF SHAN PRESENTS?

To submit your manuscript to Shan Presents, please send the first three chapters and synopsis to submissions@shanpresents.com

CPSIA information can be obtained
at www.ICGtesting.com
Printed in the USA
LVOW10s2336190118
563260LV00021B/816/P